It's not easy to get your life back after surviving The Big C. Sometimes you even have to:

1) Actually accept a date from the good-looking guy your friends maneuver back into your life. You know, the one you've been dreaming about since before your diagnosis.
2) Start a journal to prove to the world that you're getting your life back. (And maybe to prove it to yourself, too.)
3) Listen to your friends when they say it's time to lose the baseball caps you've been hiding under, even though your dad gave you those caps and not much else.
4) Stop trying to run your uncle's diner from the back room. Get out there and mingle with the customers—especially the cute ones.
5) Remember to push your knitting buddies to take their own lives back—even though you're already missing your caps and wondering if your dream guy is really your particular dream after all.

Books by Janet Tronstad

Love Inspired

**An Angel for Dry Creek* #81
**A Gentleman for Dry Creek* #110
**A Bride for Dry Creek* #138
**A Rich Man for Dry Creek* #176
**A Hero for Dry Creek* #228
**A Baby for Dry Creek* #240
**A Dry Creek Christmas* #276
**Sugar Plums for Dry Creek* #329
**At Home in Dry Creek* #371
The Sisterhood of the Dropped Stitches #385

*Dry Creek

JANET TRONSTAD

grew up on a small farm in central Montana. One of her favorite things to do was to visit her grandfather's bookshelves, where he had a large collection of Zane Grey novels. She's always loved a good story. Today Janet lives in Pasadena, California, where she is a full-time writer. In addition to writing novels, she researches and writes nonfiction magazine articles.

Janet Tronstad

The Sisterhood of the Dropped Stitches

Published by Steeple Hill Books™

STEEPLE HILL BOOKS

ISBN-13: 978-0-373-81298-1
ISBN-10: 0-373-81298-1

THE SISTERHOOD OF THE DROPPED STITCHES

This edition published by arrangement with Steeple Hill Books.

www.SteepleHill.com

Printed in U.S.A.

For where two or three are gathered together
in My name, there am I in the midst of them.
—*Matthew* 18:20

Dedicated to my friend Katherine Snyder.
Thanks for all of the encouragement.

Chapter One

A spider's life can't help being something of a mess, with all this trapping and eating flies.

—*Charlotte's Web,* E. B. White

Rebecca Snyder read this quote to us six years ago at our first Sisterhood meeting. I've had it in my journal since then, scratched in pencil on the back of a Juicy Fruit gum wrapper.

"I never thought I'd live like an insect," Rebecca said after that with a discouragement I sensed was rare for her even though I didn't know her well that first night. "But, look at me—I have way too much in common with the spider, especially all that messy part."

We were all quiet for a minute.

"At least we don't need to eat any flies," Carly Winston finally added softly. She wasn't being funny. We'd all had our share of eating strange things lately. "Chemo is bad enough."

The silence stretched even longer after that. Each one of us was thinking of the flies or the chemo or both.

Rose could barely keep us focused on knitting that night. She showed us how to hold our new # 19 needles, which are the big needles that beginners use when they learn to knit.

I wish I could say we all agreed to call ourselves the Sisterhood of the Dropped Stitches that first night, but it wouldn't be true. My name's Marilee Davidson and I have been voted to be the one to tell you how we started six years ago. I have everyone's permission to tell you how it was with us back then, and I'm writing it all down in this journal. We are seventy-five percent sure—the vote is three to one—that we will try to place this journal where others can read it so, if you're reading it now, I guess we finally all decided to let our story go forth and speak to who it will.

Anyway, the first thing you need to know is that on our first night together we couldn't agree on anything, not even a name. Rebecca—Becca for short—wanted to call us The Bald Ones although most of us hadn't become bald yet and weren't looking forward to it. I'll admit I argued with Becca over this. Only she would even *want* a name like The Bald Ones.

I thought Becca was strange at first because of the quote and the name suggestion, but I gradually came to realize that it was just the way she met life—jumping ahead to the problems. When we started, Becca was sixteen, dark-haired and vigorous. She had an opinion about everything and pounded into life even though she was sick.

Picture that bunny on television who advertises the batteries. That was Becca, only she was skinnier than the bunny—she made me promise to add that—and was smooth-skinned instead of fuzzy white. I'm adding that on my own out of simple jealousy—Becca's skin is a light olive shade and it doesn't freckle or blemish or burn like my pale, partially English skin does.

Anyway, I wish you could have seen Becca in those days. Every move she made had energy in it. Maybe that was why she believed in telling it like it is, no matter how unpleasant the "it" might be. Looking back, I think she was hoping that if she was only gut-wrenchingly honest enough about her cancer diagnosis, the sting of it would go away. As if maybe the whole thing was a pill she needed to swallow and so she was better off just gulping it down quick before the bad taste spread to the rest of her mouth.

Becca was Jewish and lived with her family down by the Fairfax district in Los Angeles. She used to say her "people" knew how to fight back, but sometimes I thought she looked scared when she said it. That didn't stop her from pounding ahead, though. That was our Becca.

Eighteen-year-old, Carly, on the other hand, was tall, blonde and serene. She didn't pound anywhere; she glided. She lived in San Marino which had to mean her family was rich even though she never said anything about money or what her parents did for work. In fact, she didn't say much about her parents at all, not even to complain about them, so I guessed they were pretty impressive.

You'd have to be around Carly to understand why she didn't go on about her parents. If her father were the president of the United States, she wouldn't mention it because she wouldn't want to make the rest of us feel bad that our dads were only ordinary men. Everyone knows it takes lots of money to live in San Marino, though, so I figured her father was president of something. I never knew how much distance there was between her bank account and the accounts of the rest of us, although I speculated about it at first.

After a while, it didn't matter. Carly was just Carly. Nothing unnerved Carly, and she never seemed to break a sweat. Out of all of us, she was the one who always wore makeup to her doctor's appointments.

Carly usually tried to make our treatment sound like a day at the spa. You might think she was in major denial, but that wasn't it. She knew what she faced right down to the numbers on her last blood test. She just always thought everything would be okay. If there was a rosy glass anywhere around, you could count on Carly to polish it up and look right through it. Carly was the one who suggested we become the Sisterhood of the Dropped Stitches.

Lizabett MacDonald, at fifteen, was the youngest member of our group. She'd lost all her hair by the time we started to meet, so I didn't know back then that her hair was light brown. All I knew was that she wore a black scarf wrapped around her head like a turban. She was so thin and her face was so white, the scarf made her look like a skeleton in mourning. When her hair grew back in, it had a tinge of red to it.

Lizabett was the only girl in a big Irish family and, by her own admission, had been born shy. She also said she was content to stay that way—shy, that is.

I don't think Lizabett was overly thrilled with her family. She said it always sounded like a freight train was going through when they sat down to have a meal together. She liked a little more quiet. She even jokingly offered to give Carly a couple of her brothers when she found out Carly had no siblings. Lizabett had three siblings, all older brothers who, according to her, stomped when a step would do.

All of Lizabett's brothers were local firefighters. Maybe because Lizabett's father had died when she was very young, she talked about her brothers a lot even though they annoyed her. She especially talked about the oldest one, whom she called "The Old Mother Hen" because he worried over her. He was always encouraging Lizabett to talk more, and it made her mad.

"I can say what I have to say when I have to say it," Lizabett told us. "The Old Mother Hen doesn't need to keep at me about it."

Of course, it wasn't true—Lizabett was too shy sometimes to even find out what she needed to know from the nurses or the lab techs—but one of the rules we'd come to abide by in the Sisterhood was that we wouldn't burst anyone's bubble if there was any way to avoid it. We all lived with enough pain; we didn't want to inflict any more on each other. If Lizabett needed to believe she was as outgoing as Queen Latifah, we would let her. So we only nodded and said The Old Mother Hen was just trying to help her.

We never pressured Lizabett to say anything. We assured her she didn't need to have an opinion about everything if she didn't want to have one.

Fortunately, Lizabett did have an opinion about our name. She voted for the Sisterhood of the Dropped Stitches because she thought we were serious about knitting and should have a name with "Stitches" in it. She liked things to be clear and identifiable, which sort of went along with her Old Mother Hen label.

As for me, I was so distraught by then that I didn't care what we called ourselves, although I do remember thinking there was some kind of cosmic justice in calling ourselves the Dropped Stitches. I mean, if you looked at our lives, you could see we were all like dropped stitches.

I used to wonder if God had been watching some all-engrossing football game on television when He made us, and that was why He missed the stitches that ended up letting cancer into our bodies. Becca had a bone tumor. Carly had Hodgkin's disease. Lizabett had a tumor in the muscle of her leg. I had breast cancer. None of our bodies had been made right. I didn't mind telling Him it was a pretty big miss when He dropped the stitches in us. The stitch He missed in me changed my life.

There is nothing like a diagnosis of breast cancer at nineteen to scare away a girl's future. I dropped out of my UCLA classes to cope with the chemo and decided to say no to dates even though I'd been fantasizing for months that the college guy who had been working the grill in my uncle's diner would ask me out—which he, Randy Parker, aka the grill guy, did the week after I got my diagnosis.

Some days it's all about the timing of things, isn't it?

The grill guy had the best eyes, sort of a blue-gray stormy night look to them, but I knew saying no was the only thing to do. I mean, this guy was a big player on the UCLA football team. When he started working at the diner that summer before his senior year, you wouldn't believe how many UCLA students came in. The students weren't all girls, but enough were that I was amazed when he asked me to see a movie with him after work one night.

I just stood and looked at him with a plate of garlic fries in my hands and a net over my hair. For a split second, I forgot about my cancer. I think I might have even had a ringing in my ears. It was one of those "light in the tunnel" kind of things. I was blinded by the fact that he'd finally really noticed me.

When I got my breath back, I remembered the cancer. Of course, he didn't know about my diagnosis—my mother was the only one who knew—but I figured he'd find out soon enough, and I didn't want him to feel awkward about the whole thing. Most guys aren't interested in a date who has to worry about a partial mastectomy and chemo-induced nausea.

Besides, what if, after he found out about the cancer, he thought he had to keep asking me out because I was sick. What kind of a guy would he be if he dumped me when I might be dying? See how complicated it could become? I didn't want to be a stone around some guy's neck. I didn't want to be anyone's charity date, either.

The light in that tunnel disappeared fast enough.

I told the grill guy I wasn't dating. Just like that I went from giving him my best come-hither smiles to cold silence. He probably thought I was weird, but at least he didn't think I was dying.

I was glad the grill guy went back to college before my diagnosis was common knowledge at my uncle's diner. At a certain point, cancer is a hard secret to keep, especially when your hair starts to fall out, but—as bad as it became—I was always grateful I didn't have to face the grill guy with the news.

Even though I was glad I didn't have to see the pity in his eyes, it still seemed unfair that I was cheated out of my chance at a date with him. He could have been my destiny, and I'd never know for sure. You know how sometimes, when you're so overwhelmed about all of the big worries, there's some small worry that you focus on and think if you could just change that one thing everything else would snap back into place? That was me and my missed date with the grill guy.

The resentment about how unfair my life had become festered in me, but it wasn't something I could talk to my doctors about, especially not when they were busy trying to save my life. It seemed I should at least be able to handle my feelings. I mean, they were only feelings—they weren't tumors. All I needed was someone to talk to about things, preferably someone who had some experience with things like this and would know what to say.

I was emphatically not talking to God on account of the dropped stitches thing, so there was no point in going to my mother's church and talking to one of the counselors there as she suggested.

I think if I hadn't already started to warm up to God, I would have taken His indifference better. Mom had become a Christian six months or so before my diagnosis and that's when the changes really started in our family. My parents had argued with each other for as long as I could remember, but mostly it was about small stuff. Granted, there was a lot of small stuff, but we all just sort of got used to the bickering.

Then Mom announced she was a Christian. Boom—just like that, she told me and Dad about it one night when we'd finished one her special roast chicken dinners. Usually, when we had roast chicken for dinner, my parents managed to get along a little better. Even Dad had to agree Mom made a great chicken dinner.

But that night, Dad wasn't thinking about dinner. He said he'd rather be married to a woman in a mental institution than a Christian, and he told Mom to stop talking nonsense. Mom said it wasn't nonsense and she wasn't going to stop. Dad didn't like that, so he said he'd rather be married to an ugly, mean-spirited woman in the largest mental institution in the world than some pigheaded, self-serving Christian who believed heaven was the answer to everything.

There was a moment of silence after he said all that. Even I was shocked at his bitterness. Then Mom said Dad would be sorry someday for saying things like that, and he should think about repenting before it was too late. Dad said he'd repent over his dead body. Mom said it was likely that was just what was going to happen.

Dad looked at us and then threw down his dinner napkin before stomping out of the room. After that, I could tell my parents weren't arguing from habit any longer.

They were arguing in earnest now, and it went on for months.

Finally, Dad moved out of the house. I never could decide if it was fortunate or unfortunate that he made his move the week after Mom and I learned about my diagnosis. Cancer was so far from my mind at that time that I couldn't figure out why the doctor had asked me to bring my mom with me for my final visit. I thought he was worried about my mom skipping a mammogram or something. I was shocked when he said I had a tumor. I was glad my mother was there even though I wasn't ready to tell anyone else about the diagnosis.

The good part of Dad's timing in moving out was that my news gave Mom something to worry about besides the state of Dad's soul, so she didn't fight with him when he said he was leaving.

The bad part, of course, was that I would have liked to have both of my parents with me when I faced the cancer. I never did have the courage to ask Mom if she'd told Dad about my cancer before he decided to leave. I never had the courage to ask him, either. I just told myself he couldn't have known when he left.

At least I still saw my dad after he moved out of the house. Uncle Lou is Dad's older brother, and so Dad would come by the diner every few months to watch sports on the big-screen television we have. Baseball was his real passion, but he watched football, too. On those nights when my dad would come by, he and I would have a cup of coffee and cheer his team to victory. Usually, he'd have a baseball cap for me from some team. He'd put the cap on my head and give me an arm-around-the-shoulder bit of a hug.

Anyway, I didn't want to take sides in the argument my parents were having, so even though I had gone to church a few times with my mother before my dad left, I didn't want to go to church with her after he left just in case he ever asked me about it. I didn't want him to think I'd chosen Mom over him.

And, if I wasn't going to go to church for real, I didn't think it was exactly fair to go to church for some kind of counseling. Besides, I had gotten cancer not long after Mom became a Christian, so I wasn't feeling too kindly toward God anyway. Wasn't He supposed to take care of people who said they were Christians? Shouldn't He have taken better care of me since Mom prayed for me and she had joined up with Him? It didn't seem fair.

But I couldn't keep all of my angry feelings inside.

So, I talked to Rose, a student counselor at the hospital. Rose was the one who first decided the four of us—me, Carly, Becca and Lizabett—needed to be in a group together. She said we should be like normal teenagers and have a club.

I remember wondering at the time just how normal she expected us to be when we were all staring death in the face. Rose had been an elementary school teacher for some years before she went back to graduate school, so she was prepared for life. Still, she looked as scared as I felt.

I suspected comforting me was worse for Rose than comforting her usual clients, because she and I had become friends in the weeks I'd known her. I had to become close to her. She was my rock. I talked to her about the things I couldn't talk to my mom about. I needed Rose. But that didn't stop me from telling her I didn't want to belong to any stupid cancer group.

"Cancer? Who said anything about a cancer group?" Rose said after a brief pause. "No, no, I'm talking about starting a knitting group. Lots of people knit these days."

I know the knitting idea just flew into Rose's head when I was so stubborn about joining a cancer group. But once she said it, the whole thing seemed to take root. Apparently, her farm-raised grandmother had taught Rose how to knit, and she was happy—maybe even relieved—to teach us. She told me later she was glad she could do something concrete with her hands to help us.

Rose's grandmother was fond of old sayings and quotes, so Rose decided one of us would bring a quote to each meeting in case we ran out of things to talk about while we sat there tangled in all of our yarn.

I had been telling Rose about the grill guy for the twentieth time when she thought of having a club. I soon learned that not being able to date some guy was the least of my troubles. I'm not sure how I would have gotten through all the chemo and the scared feelings without the Sisterhood. Before long I would have knitted those scarves with my teeth if I'd had to just so I could keep meeting with the Sisterhood.

This was almost six years ago, and we all made it.

Let me repeat that. We all made it. Three cheers. I still feel good every time I say that.

The prognosis for all of us was different, but five years was the longest time any of us had needed to wait to become officially Survivors. There hasn't been a week in all that time when we've considered stopping the Sisterhood for more than a holiday break. If it's not Thanksgiving or Christmas, every Thursday the five of us meet in The Pews—that's the name of my Uncle Lou's diner. We sit at the big table in the back room and knit.

These days, one of my favorite times is when someone brings a quote to the Sisterhood meeting. I think it was the quotes that made us turn so reflective that we decided to set some goals last year. Reaching the five-year mark was such a major thing—I can't even describe it. We couldn't think of anyway big enough to celebrate, so Rose suggested we all make a special goal for the next year—something that would show we were taking our lives back.

All I can say about those goals is that I wish I hadn't gotten caught up in the optimism and foolishly made a goal about dating. I should've known that female-male attraction can't be goaled into being. Finding the right guy to date—someone who really curls your toes, as Rose would say—should never be part of anyone's must-meet annual goals. Love doesn't work on a schedule.

Trust me on this. Let me tell you how Becca set her goal. She has always wanted to become a lawyer. She was already taking some prelaw classes at UCLA, so she set her goal as being chosen to be an intern with this local judge for next summer. That's a perfect goal—it's a clear step in a clear direction. The judge always selects two prelaw students to work with her from June to September. It's apparently a big deal because the judge is one of the best, according to Becca, who knows those kinds of things.

Getting that internship is a sensible goal, and Becca says she's sure to get it, given her grades and references. Her grandfather knows someone who knows the judge and is willing to put in a good word for her. Becca called, and the judge's law clerk is sending the acceptance letters out this week, so Becca will get hers in plenty of time for our Sisterhood deadline of next Thursday.

If it was me, I wouldn't be so confident, but Becca gets what she wants, and I have no doubt she'll get this.

If I weren't so happy in my job as Uncle Lou's partner, I would have chosen a goal to advance my career, as well.

Not that all of our goals are about jobs.

Carly decided to get a Maine coon cat. She'd always wanted a cat, she told us, but she couldn't get one because she's allergic to cats. The Maine coon cat, however, is a purebred that has different dander than other cats or something. Anyway, it has the long hair Carly likes but is still okay for people with allergies.

At first, I was skeptical. I couldn't imagine Carly having any animal with coon in its name. I mean, Carly is just so classy. But then Carly told us that this particular breed of cat is said to be descended from six house cats that Marie Antoinette sent to Wiscassett, Maine, when she was hoping to escape from France during the French Revolution.

Isn't that something? The cats were to be there to welcome Marie when she made it to the New World. Now that sounded more like Carly. She likes movie stars and royalty. She'll love having a cat whose ancestors had waited for Marie Antoinette.

Of course, the cat was not cheap. It cost Carly two thousand dollars, and it took her months to find one. In fact, she just got her cat a week or so ago. She had to fly to Seattle to pick it up.

I was happy for Carly when she met her goal. I even sent her home with a small piece of fish from the diner after our meeting last week.

Carly was the first one to meet her goal.

When we set our goals, Lizabett surprised us by saying she'd always wanted to perform in a ballet, twirling and dipping around onstage in a costume. Her eyes lit up just talking about it. Her leg had healed just fine after the surgery removing her tumor so, of course, ballet had to be her goal. She'd signed up for classes before the month was out at a community dance studio over in Sierra Madre.

Lizabett is performing next Wednesday in a production the studio is doing of *Swan Lake.* When the performance date was first being discussed, Lizabett told the other ballet students about her goal and they voted to move the production forward a few days so she could meet it. She's so excited. She showed us a picture of her costume last week—it's all white net and froth. She'll look adorable on stage.

Next Thursday is the date when the goals are due to be completed, and I'm the only one who hasn't done what I'd said I would do. You would think I would get some extra credit for writing up this description of how we started the Sisterhood, but no one seems willing to let me slide on my goal. And I haven't even come close to meeting it.

My goal is to have three dates with a man, or men, I could see myself with long-term. Carly suggested the long-term addition, and I know now I shouldn't have listened. Carly gets asked for so many dates she can be picky about long-term attraction.

I'm not Carly. If men ask me out, it's obviously not about looks. I have to rely on my personality here. My skin is not spotty, but its color is uneven—I don't have the English skin that's like fine porcelain; mine's more like thick white crockery that's been given a sturdy glaze. Plus, my lips are too thin and my cheekbones are not pronounced enough for real beauty.

Not that I'm a wreck, by any means. I look wholesome, but I'm certainly not Rose Queen material as Carly is. The point being that I need to count all of my dates—long-term and short-term and anything in between.

Even at that, I wasn't worried when I first

set the goal, because a year is a long time. How could I have known I'd procrastinate? The problem was, I didn't want to be on a manhunt. I just wanted it to happen, you know?

I think it was all the philosophizing with the quotes that wore down my good sense to the point that I even made this kind of a goal. The others brought in some quotes that made a person think anything was possible if the whole group worked on it. After we'd been bald and scared together, we didn't have any barriers left. Once we'd reached our five-year marker, anything seemed possible. I'm lucky I didn't vow to become an astronaut and fly to the moon.

Usually that kind of soaring enthusiasm is a good thing, but lately—well, at least since the big Thursday is coming up so fast—I've begun to wonder if some of those in the Sisterhood haven't grown *too* supportive of seeing me actually meet my goal. They keep saying Friday, Saturday and Sunday are all excellent date nights. I'll be doing good if they don't hurry me out of our meeting tonight with orders to find some man on the street to have coffee with me before the diner closes.

Come to think of it, there is that coffee place down the street in De Lacey Alley. There might be a busboy there who will sit down at a table with me and have a cup of coffee if I pay the bill. I wonder if that would count?

We make too much of dates in our culture anyway. In some countries, just giving a man a look would be equivalent to a date—and I've certainly *looked* at men in the past year. Don't you think that should count for something?

Chapter Two

Please understand that there is no depression in this house; we are not interested in the possibilities of defeat, they do not exist.

—Queen Victoria

Carly brought this quote to the Sisterhood one day when we were all feeling discouraged. Carly thought the queen said it when England was at war. Carly isn't keen on war, but she, of course, always picks quotes from the royals and movie stars. I wonder sometimes why she doesn't get an agent and try to get on the big screen.

Carly would be a beautiful movie star.

Besides, it would give her something to do with her days—not that she isn't already doing profitable things. She has her charities, and she's taking one or two Interior Design classes from some private school. Really, I suspect she's just marking time until she marries some nice, rich man who can support her in her San Marino lifestyle.

But until she gets married, I worry that Carly worries too much about the rest of us. Does that make sense? She just seems to take everything to heart.

Okay, so Carly's right—I have to admit I have over thirty baseball caps and have never played the game. I've watched enough games with my dad, though, so in a way, I've earned the caps. I think Carly should take that into account instead of standing beside Becca in The Pews, looking at me in that patient way she has where she waits for the other person to connect all the dots.

I hate dots.

I am getting ready to tell the two of them I'll take them to Victory Park and see if we can find a baseball game if they're so determined that I get more involved in life, but I know they aren't here about baseball or about my caps.

Carly seems willing to stand there and let me work on connecting the dots, but Becca is clearly ready to burst. Dots are too slow for her.

"You're never going to meet any men unless you stop hiding out here!"

Becca makes her pronouncement and flings her backpack down on the top of the counter. I wince, even though I know the backpack is too light to do any damage. The mahogany counter is Uncle Lou's pride and joy. It almost kills him to let people eat their sandwiches at it; but since The Pews is an upscale hamburger diner, he has no choice about letting paying customers put their elbows on the counter.

The backpack is another matter, even though I know it is too soft to do any damage and Becca is a particular favorite with Uncle Lou because she watches football with him on the diner's television most Monday nights during the season—better than that, she actually understands the game and can argue with him about the strategies of the teams.

"Not that you shouldn't still work here—The Pews is great." Becca amends her opinion. "It's just that you need to meet more men someplace."

"If you look around here, you'll see men." I sweep the place with my arm. It is relatively empty except for a couple of regulars who don't even bother looking up from their coffee. These regulars might be in their sixties, but they are definitely men. They even have beards.

It is obvious that the reason Becca has come early today is to talk to me about the men I haven't met and the dates I haven't had—which, believe me, can be a long conversation. Carly, on the other hand, probably came to temper Becca's enthusiasm. Carly's the peacemaker in our group, and is never willing to see the rest of us quarrel.

Speaking of which—the Sisterhood will be meeting in a few hours. Uncle Lou keeps a running reservation for the group in the back room of The Pews for Thursday nights from seven to ten. He even usually brings us cups of herbal tea and biscotti and makes a big deal about it being on the house. Everyone should have an Uncle Lou in their life.

Of course, Uncle Lou isn't here right now. It's four o'clock in the afternoon, and he is out following some lead on a temporary grill operator. I don't know what kind of a genius he's lining up. Only a few people have experience in old grills like the one we have. Uncle Lou was a little vague about where he was going, but that is Uncle Lou's way. He doesn't like being bothered with details and schedules.

Of course, that's why he turned that part of the business over to me years ago. I may not be in the front part of the diner all the time, but I don't think it's accurate to say I don't meet people.

"I'm not hiding. There are 235 people who come through these doors on an average day. I know. I do the books."

The diner has a whole row of windows that look out over Colorado Boulevard. This is "the street" in Pasadena since it is the one that the Rose Parade goes down on the beginning of every year. Uncle Lou has had some sort of restaurant on this spot along the parade route since long before any of the upscale restaurants that now crowd the street opened their doors.

"We're just a couple of blocks away from Kevin Costner's restaurant," I say. That always distracts Carly. J Lo's sister has a place, too, but I don't add that. "This is a happening place."

I started waiting tables at Uncle Lou's when I was in high school. For the past six years, I've worked here full-time and I've multiplied the income from the diner five times over. I added avocado to the menu, antique pews to the decor and college students to the waitstaff. Then I changed the name from Lou's to The Pews, and it became a trendy place, but not so trendy that Uncle Lou lost his regulars. It was a brilliant compromise between old and new.

This past year Uncle Lou made me a partner, and now he goes around saying he is so rich he's thinking of retiring early. I do the books, so I know he can do it. Not that he ever will. He loves this diner. This year, though, he is planning to take a vacation for the first time in years—that is, if he can find someone who can handle that grill while he's gone.

I should have learned how to use that particular grill years ago, but Uncle Lou is a bit of a sexist when it comes to the grill. He says the old thing gives off too much heat for a woman and it's a job for a man.

What he doesn't say is that our grill at The Pews is ancient and temperamental and should have been replaced years ago. Uncle Lou is attached to the thing, though. He swears the new grills don't work as well—something about it being hot and steady at the same time instead of just one or the other.

But that isn't why Carly and Becca are here. I look up at them to see if they're still stuck on their topic. They are.

"...in the back room. You do the books in the back room," Carly points out gently when she sees my attention is back with them.

"It's not a back room, it's an office."

Becca rolls her eyes. Carly's approach is always too subtle for her.

"It's not even the *front* back room, where somebody might see you. It's the room behind the back room," Becca grumbles. "You might as well be home in your pajamas for all the people who see you."

"I don't think I need to be on display. I

don't want to be obvious about this meeting-a-man thing anyway. Besides, I'm up here tonight taking orders. You don't get more visible than that. In fact, if Annie doesn't get here soon, I'll miss our meeting and be on view up here all night."

Annie is one of The Pew waitresses. Chrissy is the other waitress, but she isn't due in tonight.

"That's not the same," Becca says. "You need to do something."

"We have ads out so we can hire some more waitresses."

"Then you'll never leave your office," Becca says as she sits down on one of the bar stools at the counter. The bottoms of the bar stools are brass-plated and give the whole place the kind of class it needs to match up with the mahogany counter. Becca moves her backpack off the counter and swings it down to her feet. Red mohair yarn sticks out of one of the side pockets.

I smile when I see the yarn. Mohair is hard to knit with because it can get all tangled up. "You always do need a challenge."

"I just feel like we've come so far," Becca

says. "Too far to give up now. You were so brave with your surgery, and the follow-up treatment went well, too. You need to get past everything and meet a nice guy. And now's the time. You're the only one who might not meet your goal."

I know Becca wants to just pound through any obstacles. That's what we did when we were all so sick. She helped me get through my partial mastectomy and the reconstruction that followed. I, more than any of the others, owe her for her determination. It kept me going through some dark days. It upheld me back then even though it feels like overkill now.

I reach for one of the cloths I use to polish the counter and give the counter a few rubs. "If it makes you feel any better, I'm fine with my body. I'm not holding back. Besides, the surgeons did such a good job, you can hardly tell I had surgery. And I'm not a recluse. A person can't be a recluse on Colorado Boulevard. Thousands of people walk down this street every week—more if you're talking the Rose Parade."

Becca took one of the other cloths and began to rub the counter, as well. "A person can be a recluse anywhere if they want to be one. When was the last time you went anywhere that wasn't for work?"

"I'm trying to get everything done so I can go to our Dropped Stitches meeting tonight. That's not work."

"You know what we mean." Carly enters the conversation as she begins to arrange the salt and pepper shakers on the tray the evening crew will use to reset the tables in an hour or so. "We're worried about you."

All of the members of the Sisterhood know their way around Uncle Lou's place. They've even waited tables a time or two when The Pews has been busy and short-staffed.

"I'm fine, Carly. Fine. Six years fine."

Becca grimaces as she rubs a bigger circle on the counter. She puts her whole body into the polishing motion. "If you're so fine, why haven't you met your goal?"

"Do we have to meet every single goal?"

"Of course." Becca stops rubbing. She sounds surprised, as if she hasn't even thought of the possibility of failure. "We've met them all so far. We can meet this one, too. It isn't like you to miss a goal."

I know how Becca feels. She's pumped. For a long time, I had that same kind of desperate need to have everything under control. The future was so cloudy we just grabbed one goal at a time and hung on to it as we worked our way through the pain. But did that mean we had to live the rest of our lives with that same need to have everything come out the way we planned it?

"I think maybe I picked the wrong goal," I finally say.

"It's not the wrong goal—it's the absolute right one for you." Becca starts wiping the counter again. "Besides, you can't change goals now. You just need encouragement. We all know you'd like to start dating again. Who wouldn't?"

"I could learn Spanish instead. That's a skill I could use at the diner."

"Maybe you could date someone who speaks Spanish," Carly offers. She has finished the salt and pepper shakers and is working on the small bowls with red pepper flakes now.

"I'll date when I meet the right guy." I appeal to Carly. "I'm sure you didn't just buy the first coon cat you saw when you decided you wanted one."

"Maine coon cat," Carly corrects me. "It's French."

"You've had a year to look around," Becca says stubbornly. "Carly managed to find that French cat, and they're a rare breed. If she can find a rare cat, you should be able to find a perfectly ordinary man to have coffee with. You don't even need to ask the guy his pedigree—he can just be a guy who's single."

"I've been busy."

"There's nothing wrong with being selective," Carly says just as if she hadn't heard me say I was busy. "No one is saying you have to rush out and put an ad in the paper or anything. You can take it slow."

"But not this slow," Becca clarifies. "You've got to get three dates in a week."

"I can't help it if I haven't met anyone I want to date."

"You know, the problem might be more than that," Carly says.

I tense up. Everybody thinks I have a problem with my body since I've had my partial mastectomy, but it's not true.

"Remember how you were when you were learning to knit?" Carly says to me. "Every time you dropped a stitch, you had to unravel your yarn back to the place where you made the mistake. Even when Rose taught us how to fix a dropped stitch without going back, you always unraveled."

"I wanted to be sure."

Carly nods. "Maybe it's that way with you and men. Maybe you need to go back to that guy you liked so much when you stopped dating. What was his name?"

"You mean the grill guy? I can't go back to being nineteen and all bothered by some guy who worked at the diner."

I'm relieved this isn't about my body image, but I'm still not so sure about the direction Carly's taking. I know I did my share of wailing over the unfairness of cancer and my missed date with the grill guy, so I'm not surprised Carly remembers it. But that was a long time ago. I'm not still infatuated with the grill guy.

"Why can't you go back?" Carly asks. "Didn't you always say that it was the grill guy who made you feel there was a dropped stitch in your life?"

"Yes, but..." I shook my head. "I mean, it's not like I *knew* him or anything."

"Sure you did. He was working the grill here, and you were waiting tables on the weekends," Becca says. "Your shifts must have overlapped."

"Well, of course, I talked to him, but 'make it two burgers, with everything on them' doesn't mean we had much conversation."

"He asked you out," Becca says.

"Six years ago!"

"What about those eyes of his—the ones that looked like a storm cloud coming?"

"Just because I noticed his eyes, it doesn't mean I want to date him now. Why, I don't even know where he is. He could be living in Australia, for all I know."

There is a moment's silence, and Becca and Carly exchange a quick glance.

"He lived in Hollywood when he worked here," Becca finally says.

"Really?" I completely stop rubbing down the counter. I never knew that. I'm starting to have a bad feeling in my bones.

"I kind of asked your Uncle Lou about him—just in a general way," Becca says. "I didn't say anything about his eyes or you dating him or anything. I just asked if he remembered the guy who worked the grill that summer when you got cancer."

"Becca would never actually betray a confidence and say anything about you and the grill guy," Carly quickly assures me.

Now I understood why Carly came with Becca this afternoon. They are worried I will be upset about Becca stepping into my business. I think about it for a couple of seconds before I realize they don't need to worry. When someone has stood shoulder to shoulder with you in the wars, it's hard to get upset if they step on your little toe later. Besides, I've wasted enough emotion over that grill guy to last anyone a lifetime. I don't need to make a big deal of him now.

"It's okay. It doesn't matter if you found out where the grill guy lived. He is so not the point anymore."

"You're sure?" Becca asks. She looks a little anxious.

I give her a smile and a nod. "It's all history."

Carly and Becca exchange another one of those looks.

That funny feeling in my bones is growing.

"But you wouldn't mind seeing him, would you? I mean, if you walked into him on the street or something?" Becca asks.

"I don't think that would happen," I say. "I'm sure we don't walk down the same streets anymore. He might have lived in Hollywood when he was a student, but he's probably gone back to Ohio or someplace by now."

Carly clears her throat.

Becca squares her shoulders. "He might be closer than that. See, your uncle Lou—well, I think he tracked the guy down and he's meeting with him right about now. Your uncle is asking him to take over the grill while he goes on vacation."

Becca took a sudden interest in the floor.

"Oh." I see now. My life is a house of mirrors. I look one way only to have to look the other way to try and see the real picture. Everything has shifted.

"I don't want you to be angry," Becca adds with a quick upward glance toward me. "I know that sometimes I get carried away. But

I truly didn't think it would be a bad thing if your Uncle Lou called the grill guy up and asked him to come back to work for a few weeks."

I look at the two faces in front of me. We've battled cancer together. What is one grill guy compared to all that?

I take a deep breath. "I'm not angry."

The feeling in my bones has settled into stiffness in my neck.

"Good," Carly says as she puts a hand on my shoulder and makes a massaging motion up my neck. She hasn't forgotten that stress settles there for me.

"I am maybe a little concerned, however," I admit.

Becca nods. "Don't worry. I would never say anything to the guy himself about dating you."

"With any luck, he won't even remember me," I say. Carly's neck massage is already making me feel better. And I'm right. The grill guy won't remember me. He's had six years of people pass through his life since that summer—I can't even begin to speculate on how many dates that has been for him.

What am I thinking? “He’s probably married by now anyway.”

Carly and Becca both look surprised. I am glad they hadn’t thought of that, either. One thing we have in common in the Sisterhood is that we all had six years carved out of our lives. We’re out of step with the larger world in the same way. While other people had been doing normal things like getting married, we’d been waiting to see if we’d live. Our clocks are all slightly askew. Maybe that’s why we’ve made so much of our goals. Time has passed us by for too long.

“We’ll find you three dates someplace else,” Becca says a little too quickly. “Maybe one of those matchmaking sites on the Internet.”

“That doesn’t sound safe,” Carly says as she stops the massage on my neck. “She can’t go out with a stranger.”

“Maybe if I had an e-mail exchange with them that could count as a date,” I offer.

Becca frowns. I can tell she is tempted. She wants to wrap up these goals so there are no loose ends. But she’s always been a player who insists on being fair. “Well, maybe if it was a long and significant e-mail exchange. No, 'hi, how are you?' kind of a thing."

"I can do long e-mails."

"And personal. You know, with information about you. What you do. Your hobbies. That kind of thing," Becca says.

"Maybe even your experience with cancer," Carly adds. "And not just the medical stuff—the emotions, too."

The stress has left my neck, and the funny feeling in my bones is long gone. I can do some e-mails. I don't know why I didn't think of it before.

Everything is going to be okay. I am feeling generous toward Becca and Carly. Maybe they are right to give me a little nudge. A few e-mails won't be bad. And, if I'm on a matchmaking site, there should be lots of choices in men to e-mail. In the meantime, there's that coffee place in De Lacey Alley. I've got it made.

I, Marilee Davidson, will have my three dates. Just wait and see. I'm home free.

Chapter Three

Love never gives. It only lends.
—Chinese proverb

I found this ancient Chinese proverb one day and brought it to a Sisterhood meeting when we were all doing our chemo routine. We figured it meant that nothing in life is guaranteed. We all knew that fact too well. Still, it was kind of nice to have some old Chinese man from a long time ago agree with us.

Not that we knew it was a man who said it. We sat and talked about it, but couldn't decide if the one who wrote the proverb was a man or a woman. Carly thought it sounded more like a man.

Of course, it might have been a woman who said it and a man who finally wrote it down. Lizabett was the one who pointed that out—she'd turned sixteen and had another argument with The Old Mother Hen—this time because he'd told her to be careful driving in the rain. It would be just like him, she said, to follow her around and write down what she said.

I know you're dying to hear about Uncle Lou and the grill guy, but all I can say is that you need to wait in line. Several hours have passed, and Uncle Lou just got back to the diner. Becca, Carly and I are curious, too. Of course, we don't want to make a big deal of anything in front of Uncle Lou. At least, that's what I'm telling myself. Becca is giving me a nudge and a meaningful look. She apparently sees things differently.

"Becca said you were seeing about someone to work the grill for you," I finally say to Uncle Lou after he's put on his white bib apron and greeted the regulars by name.

Just to look casual, I clear away the plates that one of the counter customers left.

Uncle Lou grunts as he pulls down a glass from the overhead rack and pours himself some iced tea from the pitcher we keep behind the counter. "Yeah, it might work out. Randy Parker—remember him? He's the college guy who worked the grill here that summer…."

Uncle Lou looks at me and then looks away as though he doesn't want to remind me about the summer I got my cancer diagnosis. Cancer is a conversation stopper, all right.

Fortunately, Uncle Lou continues, "Ah, anyway, Randy's thinking about doing it. He'll let me know. He's got his own place now down on Melrose—some great hangout diner that just got written up in the *L.A. Times* sports section—can you believe it? A write-up like that is gold. Anyway, Randy says he has a fond spot in his heart for our diner here. Said we were his inspiration. So he might just do it. He's one of the few guys I've seen who can really handle that grill. Don't know why I didn't think of him before—if Becca hadn't reminded me of him, I'd still be trying to find someone…."

Uncle Lou's words trail off as he reaches

for some of the unshelled peanuts we keep in little bowls on the counter.

Becca lifts her eyebrow to me, but as far as I'm concerned, that's all I'm going to ask. Finally, she grins at me.

"So," Becca says to my uncle as she picks her backpack up from the floor by the counter stool. "This grill guy won't be too busy with his kids or anything, will he? I mean to work nights?"

My uncle stops cracking the peanut he has in his hand. "Kids? He didn't say anything about kids."

"So he's probably not married?" Becca asks.

Uncle Lou shrugs. "Didn't ask."

Just then Annie comes in, full of apologies for being late for her shift. Uncle Lou and I both wave her apology away. We know she carries a full load of classes and can't always coordinate her schedule. That's always an issue with student employees, but we like to hire them anyway. Uncle Lou says they keep the place young.

Usually, we have a male student who works the grill some and can spell Uncle

Lou, but we don't at the moment. Besides, Uncle Lou doesn't want to leave a student in charge of the grill even if we do find someone to train before he goes on vacation.

Becca adjusts her backpack over her shoulders and looks at Uncle Lou. She's like a pit bull when she has a question. There's no stopping her. "But you'll need to ask eventually, won't you? I mean, to find out who to notify if there's an emergency or something."

By now Uncle Lou has chewed up his peanuts and he gives Becca a long look. "You interested in this guy? I didn't think you knew him."

Becca has the grace to blush. At least, I think it's a blush—her normal olive skin is rosier than usual. "No, I'm not interested. And I don't know him. I was just wondering about—" I can see her searching for something sensible to say. Finally, she finds it "—employment laws as they relate to married restaurant workers—that's it—employment laws."

Uncle Lou nods as if he thinks Becca has made sense. "Of course, I forgot. But I can't ask him if he's married—isn't that against some hiring rule they have nowadays?"

Uncle Lou looks at me. Following the rules and regulations is my department so I remind him, "It's always best not to ask marital status. Or someone's age or religious status, either."

Uncle Lou nods. "Can't hardly ask anything."

"I suppose you do find out, though," Becca says. "When you ask about tax withholding and everything?"

I nod and give Becca a warning look. "Usually we do know, but that doesn't mean we can ask or that anyone's obligated to tell us."

That seems to satisfy Becca.

There's over an hour until it's time for the Sisterhood meeting. I have to finish the accounting for the day, so Becca and Carly take off to do some shopping, and I go into my office. I look around when I shut the door. It's not a large room, but I've never noticed just how small it is before.

I have a calendar of British castles on one wall. I've always wanted to stay in an old castle—my father is half-English and someday I'm going to trace our ancestors back in case we have any family castles in the distant past. That's the extent of the dreamy stuff in my office. The rest is business. I have a metal bookcase on the other wall. There is a small narrow window and my desk on the third wall. I have a straight-back chair beside my desk as well as an office chair in front of it. When the door closes, I have a long mirror on the back of the door.

Maybe Becca and Carly are right, I think to myself. My office had been a much-needed place of refuge when I was sick. Even on my good days back then, I didn't want to be around people. I was happy to escape to this room and work with numbers and suppliers. People I talked to on the phone didn't need to see my face, and I liked that.

No one just passing through could see me and ask me if I was sick, thinking I just had a bad cold. I never knew what to say when people did that. Of course I was sick. I was almost dying. But strangers didn't want to hear that, and I didn't want to tell them. They were just being polite; they didn't need to be brought down with my story. Still, I could hardly lie and say I wasn't sick, so I ended up awkwardly mumbling something about it not being contagious.

So, no, I didn't want to be around people.

I didn't have any pictures of people on my desk. I'd thought at one time about putting a picture of me and Mom on the desk, but I worried that sometime, when Dad stopped in to watch a game, he would want to see my office. If that happened, I didn't want him to see a picture of me and my mom sitting there without him.

I did have one picture, taken when I was about ten, of the three of us together. I had framed it and put it on my desk for several days when I first set up my office, but I was even more uncomfortable with that one because it seemed desperate to have to go back that many years to find a picture of us all together and smiling. So I put the picture in my bottom drawer and it's been there ever since, sitting next to the old stapler that doesn't work anymore.

These days I'm not exactly hiding from people in my office, but I'm not out there meeting anyone, either.

Maybe it is time for some changes.

I look in the mirror on the back of the door. It's a plain mirror with cardboard backing and a metal rim around it. The first thing I see is my hair sticking out from under my baseball cap. My hair grew back a long time ago, and while it is fine instead of coarse the way it used to be, it's good, healthy brown hair. I used to love having long hair, but now I keep it short. Half of the time, I chop away at it myself. It hardly seems to matter if it's styled or not when I usually wear a baseball cap over it.

I love my baseball caps.

The caps were as close as my dad and I came to talking about the effects of the chemo. He never said anything when he gave me the caps, but every few months or so he'd show up with a new one and put it on my head. Even though he never gave me much of a hug after giving me the cap, I always felt better—as if maybe the cap was his way of saying he cared about what I was facing with the chemo.

My hair is doing fine now, but I keep wearing the caps.

Maybe I *am* stuck in cancer-defense mode. Maybe I do need to take more chances in life, including meeting more men.

I meant what I said to Becca and Carly about feeling fine about my body now. But that doesn't mean my body hasn't changed some. I'm still not sure about me and men in any intimate sense. Maybe I *have* been reluctant to date.

I think about all of that for a minute, and then I take off the baseball cap I am wearing and lay it on a corner of my desk. My hair is flat, of course, but I use my fingers to comb through it a little in front of the mirror on my door. I never thought I'd feel so strange without a cap on my head.

I look at myself again in the mirror. My hair doesn't look great, but it doesn't look as bad as I thought it might. It wouldn't hurt to wear some lipstick, either. My lips are thin, but if they have some color, they won't get lost in my face. I look in my top desk drawer. I find a tube of lip gloss and put that on my lips. It doesn't give them any color, but it does make them look a little fuller.

I'll need to stop by the mall soon and get some lip liner—it wouldn't hurt to get some eye makeup, too, since my eyes will be more noticeable if I give up the baseball caps.

And, of course, there's moisturizer and foundation. It didn't seem worth the trouble of worrying about moisturizer when I was sick, so I gave it up. But now that old age is a possibility again, I should think about it. I look at my face closely in the mirror. I see two lines that could be forming beside my eyes. I need to get some moisturizer and start using it.

I stare at my face, looking for more fine lines, for a while. Then, I tell myself I can't spend the whole afternoon looking in the mirror.

I sit down at my desk and get to work. I finish doing the bookkeeping for the diner, and then I eat a sandwich.

I take my time, but I'm still the first one to the meeting room.

Usually, during the Sisterhood meetings we're so busy we don't notice the people out front in The Pews eating and laughing and having a good time. There are wood floors throughout the diner so a person does hear footsteps when other people walk around. I can usually gauge the number of customers in The Pews by the noise level. But generally we don't care if a party is going on outside;

we in the Sisterhood have our own thing going on inside our room.

There are French doors leading from the main room to the back room, and those French doors have windows. The doors don't stop all of the noise, but they do give us a feeling of privacy. There are gauze curtains we can draw over the French doors if we want, but we usually just leave the windows clear.

I like looking through the door's windows and seeing the shine of the brass rack hanging from the ceiling over the mahogany counter. The rack holds two hundred water goblets and other glasses. The glasses gleam in the soft light that comes from the electric sconces on the walls and the Tiffany lamps that hang over the tables.

The windows we see through to the outside also let the customers out there look in at us. I've wondered once in a while what the people at the counter think about the five of us sitting around the table in the back room with our heads bent over our knitting. The table and chairs are all antique oak pieces. The walls have delicate ivory wallpaper with embossed gold drawings on it. There's a grandfather clock in one corner, and several green plants on a stand in another.

Uncle Lou redecorated the room when we first started meeting in it all those years ago. Before that time, it had an old pool table and television in it. He thought it should be more like a living room for us.

We've never even considered meeting anywhere else, although some of the Sisterhood have to drive for an hour or so to get here.

We have a ritual with our meetings. We greet each other when we arrive, but we don't talk much at first. We knit for a half hour or so—that quiets our nerves. It's almost like meditation. Then we have a quote if anyone has brought one. And then we open everything up to talk.

This order of things has taught us the value of silence.

Tonight, though, we don't start with silence.

"Your hair," Carly says with a smile when she looks at me. "I can see it."

Carly and Becca both come into the room

with shopping bags. Rose is already seated at the table, and I see Lizabett coming in the outer door to the diner.

"It's pretty flat," I say. To tell the truth, since I took off my cap an hour ago, I'm beginning to worry that my hair isn't bouncing back like it used to. There's no lift to it. Maybe my hair has been permanently flattened because of me wearing caps for so long. I have my knitting in my hand, and I put it down on the table so I can go give everyone a hug.

"A good trim will take care of that," Becca says as she hugs me.

"Her head has a nice shape for short hair," Rose adds from where she sits at the table. Rose doesn't make it to all of our meetings, but we love it when she comes. She puts down her knitting, too, and stands to greet everyone.

Becca hugs Rose, while Carly gives me a hug. "Your hair's a good color."

Lizabett opens the French doors and steps into the room just then. There is a burst of noise from outside when she swings the door wide and relative silence when she closes it.

"Look at her hair," Becca says to Lizabett.

I reach out to hug Lizabett, and she tells me how nice I look.

Pretty soon everyone has hugged everyone else.

Then Carly sits down and pulls out her knitting needles. The rest of us follow her lead.

Over the years, the tools we use for knitting have changed. When we first started with our thick #19 needles, we were all so scared about our lives we could barely get the needles to do anything we wanted. In those days, I literally forced myself to think of nothing else except the needle in my hand and the stitch I needed to make.

Before long, I realized what a gift it was to be able to concentrate on knitting. It was the only time in my life back then that I didn't worry.

Now we all use different kinds of needles and don't even think about our hands. We use this time to focus on the group. There's something satisfying about looping the yarn around just so. The rest of our lives might be messy, but it makes us all feel good to see our progress with our knitting needles. It's easy to see when we drop a stitch, and we know that if we follow the patterns, our stitches will make what we want them to make.

There are not a lot of decisions to be made when we're knitting and, because of that, we all relax.

We have different skeins of yarn on the table.

I'm making a scarf from a heavy gray fisherman's wool for Uncle Lou's birthday next month. It's a surprise. He thinks I'm making the scarf for my dad for Christmas. When Uncle Lou brings in the tea—which he hasn't done yet tonight—he always says what a manly color the gray yarn is and how fine it will look around some gentleman's neck at Christmas. Then he winks at me and says he's noticed how well it would go with my dad's eyes. I just smile at him mysteriously and say it's a surprise.

I'm not the only one who's knitting something unusual.

Becca, as you know, has that red mohair yarn, and she says it's a sweater for herself. But it's larger than she wears, especially in the shoulders, and I've wondered if it's not for some guy she knows.

But Becca hasn't mentioned anyone, and she would tell the world if she was dating; not because she would be bragging, but simply because she believes in telling things the way they are. She wouldn't even think of keeping a secret like that from us. Besides, mohair isn't the yarn one would use for a man's sweater, so I must be imagining things. Either that or Becca is unaware of what she's doing. Now that's a thought.

Anyway, Rose is making an afghan for an elderly cousin of hers who lives on a farm in Upper Michigan. The afghan dips and sways and is being made out of an extra-weight brown and green yarn. Rose is using a tight knit so the afghan will be warm in those cold winter blizzards that people have in that area.

Carly is knitting a cream-colored scarf with some kind of delicate yarn. The whole thing feels almost like velvet.

Lizabett is—or has been—knitting herself a pink hat out of a lightweight yarn. I think it might be something to wear when she practices her ballet, but she hasn't said what the hat is for yet.

Something is wrong with Lizabett tonight. She has already dropped several stitches and she keeps looking through the windows in the French doors as though she's expecting to see something out in the main part of The Pews.

I'm not the only one who notices that Lizabett is not herself. I see some of the others glancing thoughtfully at her, as well. One thing I have learned about Lizabett, however, is that she is private—probably the most private one of us all. I think it comes from having all of those outgoing brothers around when she was growing up.

"How's the pattern coming?" Rose finally asks as Lizabett sets down her knitting needles in frustration. "We can adjust it if it's not working."

"It's not the pattern," Lizabett says as she bites at her lip.

"If you're hungry, I could go fix you something." I say, wondering if maybe Lizabett skipped dinner.

We all hear an increase in the noise level out at the main counter, but Lizabett is the first one to look up to see what is happening.

"I wonder if that's the grill guy," Becca

says as she stands up to look out the windows into the main room.

"*Your* grill guy?" Lizabett turns and looks at me with something like horror on her face.

I guess I hadn't quite realized how much I'd talked about that poor guy. "He's not *my* grill guy. He's just someone who worked the grill in the diner here the summer I got my diagnosis."

"But he's here?" Lizabett squeaks out another question. "Now?"

"I think so," Becca says. "That must be him."

We always keep the lighting a little dim in The Pews, but we never go really dark with it. Becca keeps looking out that glass as if she can't quite make out what she's seeing. "Wait a minute. Those guys are in uniforms."

"Well, it's not the grill guy then. But it's no big deal," I say. The Pews is located in Old Town Pasadena. The police station isn't that far away, and the officers frequently come in to get something to eat after their shifts. "You've seen cops here before."

"Yeah, but not ones coming back here," Becca whispers as she quickly moves to her chair.

I don't see how Becca can think the men walking toward the French doors haven't already seen her.

"They're not supposed to—" Lizabett says as she bites at her lip again. "That is—I told them—"

I take my eyes off of Becca and look at Lizabett. Lizabett wears her hair long, and when she hangs her head down, it's hard to see her face.

"You know these cops?" I ask Lizabett. If anyone else were acting so flustered, I would think one of the cops had written her a speeding ticket. But Lizabett would never speed.

"They're not cops," Lizabett says. The color is still high on her face, but she does lift her head and look at us. "They're firefighters. They're my brothers. I thought since you only have a week left to meet your goal—"

"*What?*" I am astonished. Lizabett is matchmaking for me. I would expect that from Becca and Carly, but not from Lizabett.

"Way to go," Becca says as she gives Lizabett the thumbs up signal. "We'll get Marilee to her goal yet."

"I didn't know the grill guy was coming

back," Lizabett whispers to me in soft apology as the French doors start to open. "I wouldn't have asked my brothers if I thought your grill guy was coming back."

"He's not *my* grill guy," I say.

"Oh," Becca says quietly.

The door fully opens, and I can understand why Becca is now speechless.

There stand three strong, tall men. They fill the doorway. None of them are *GQ* handsome, but all of them look as if they could wrestle *GQ* handsome to the ground and not even break a sweat doing it. Lizabett always made her brothers sound like annoying teddy bears. These are no teddy bears.

Where do I begin? For a second, I wonder if the warm glow around them is my imagination, but then I realize that the reason they have that golden glow surrounding them is because the light is reflecting off of the stuff one of the men has in his arms. It looks like golden-white straw.

"I brought you your wings," the man says to Lizabett as he holds out a swath of fabric. "Since when do they put these colored fiber-optic strands on wings? They reflect like crazy."

"It's a night scene, and people need to see the swans," Lizabett says as she stands up and walks toward the man with the fabric.

"Well, they'll see you all over Sierra Madre in these."

Lizabett's ballet performance is being held in a small community theatre in Sierra Madre. There hasn't been a group using that theatre for several years now, so I am glad Lizabett's dance class can use it. I bought a ticket for the production when they first went on sale.

The man drops the fabric into Lizabett's arms. "The guy who delivered it to Mom's place asked her to tell you to call your ballet teacher ASAP."

The two men who weren't talking to Lizabett were looking at the rest of us.

"Call her about what?" Lizabett asks. "I already got the news about our dress rehears-al."

The man shrugs. "If you were still living with Mom, you would have been there when he delivered the message and could have asked him. That's where you should be living anyway. That way Mom can look after you."

"I'm fine," Lizabett says. "I can look out for myself."

Lizabett moved out of her family's home last year about this time even though she needs to work a part-time job to do it since she's going to college full-time. I could understand why her brother would worry about her, but I also understand Lizabett's need to have some independence. All of the Sisterhood agrees on this. Just because we've been sick it doesn't mean we want to live our lives wrapped in cotton balls. I plan to move out of my mom's house this fall, when I will have saved up enough money for a down payment on a small condo. I'm glad Lizabett had the courage to move into her own place, as well.

I notice that Lizabett's wings lost some of their fiber-optic strands, and they are caught on her brother's dark blue uniform. Her brother's not paying any attention to his uniform, though. He's looking around the room at everyone in it.

It takes a minute to see the family resemblance between Lizabett and her brothers. The brothers all have dark hair, but the one who carried in the wings has clear blue eyes like Lizabett. His, of course, have dark eyelashes around them, and Lizabett has light brown ones.

"Oh, let me introduce everyone," Lizabett says. She is a little flushed now that everyone's eyes are on her.

"This is Gregory—Gregory MacDonald." Lizabett points to the man closest to the door. He looks like the youngest of the brothers.

Gregory nods.

"And this is Aaron MacDonald," Lizabett says as she nods toward the other man, who is also close to the door.

Aaron smiles.

"And this is Quinn." Lizabett gestures toward the man who had given her the costume. "Quinn MacDonald, my oldest brother."

Quinn smiles and gives a slight nod. "Also known in Lizabett's circles as The Old Mother Hen."

Lizabett blushes. "Well, you do hover."

Quinn grins. "I do that sometimes."

"Which one is the one you were telling us about?" Aaron finally says to Lizabett.

I feel my heart stop. How mortifying is this—Lizabett must have told her brothers I have a dating goal. This will teach me to procrastinate.

"Marilee is the one with the collection of baseball caps," Lizabett says in a hurry. "I haven't asked her yet if you can borrow them, but—"

Ah, so she didn't tell them about the goal. Thank you, Lizabett.

Aaron smiles at me and says, "We've got a crisis at our station. The guys are working with underprivileged kids in Altadena—setting up a kid's baseball team. I was hoping we could borrow your caps for our team tryouts this Saturday. Just to put on a display table with maybe a little something about the teams. It's to inspire the kids to think about what sports can do for their lives."

I had never thought of my caps as a collection before, although it is true that I have a cap of most of the major baseball teams. I hesitate a minute. I've never lent my caps out before. "Will you take care of them?"

"You're welcome to come with me to guard them if you'd like," Quinn offers with a smile. "We could use some more women to help get the girls interested."

"Why, that would be nice."

I look over at Becca. She is giving me a thumbs-up sign.

"We could go have a cup of coffee afterward or something," Quinn says.

"That would be nice." I am feeling pretty good. That's one date.

"Well, I drink coffee, too," Gregory says as he steps farther into the room and gives Lizabett a hug. "And I've been wanting to talk to one of your Sisterhood buddies."

"You don't need to check up on me," Lizabett says. "Quinn does enough of that for everyone."

"Who's checking up on you?" Gregory says. "Maybe I want to get a few pointers on how to knit."

Lizabett rolls her eyes.

Gregory looks directly at me. "How about it? Can I buy you a cup of coffee some night soon?"

It's the second date that does it. What are

the odds that two men would walk into our Sisterhood meeting and both want to have coffee with me? I glance at Aaron, and he's frowning a little bit, as though he's wondering when to jump in with his own offer for coffee.

"Do you like movies?" Aaron finally says as he gives me a smile.

Okay, that's definitely the last clue.

"Thanks," I say. "But you guys don't need to do this. It's my fault—"

Two things happened at once right then to interrupt me.

Carly's cell phone rings and someone knocks, rather loudly, on the French doors to our room.

Lizabett is closest to the doors and opens them.

Another guy comes into the room, only this guy makes my heart stop. I would know those stormy eyes anywhere.

"They said out there that you guys might know where Lou is," the guy says.

It is the grill guy.

"Sorry to barge in like this," the grill guy says when no one answers right away. I'm not sure any of us *can* answer. We are stunned. "It's just that I'm parked at a meter and I want to get back to my car."

"If Lou's not in the kitchen, try the bookstore next door. He sometimes goes there to get a newspaper," I say, and my voice doesn't creak nearly as much as I expect it to. "Or, if you want, I could give him a message for you."

"Thanks. Tell him Randy says yes, he'll do it," the guy says as he turns to leave the room.

Even Becca needs to swallow before we go on.

I hear Carly speaking softly on her cell phone.

"Did anyone see his ring hand?" Becca asks before she seems to realize there are three single men in the room. Becca looks at them with a moment's embarrassment, but then recovers. "Oh, Lou was wondering if the burn on the guy's hand healed."

"The guy's going to work the grill when Uncle Lou goes on vacation," I add nervously.

"To Florida," Lizabett adds for good measure.

"Oh, no," Carly says in a voice so non-Carly that we all look at her. She's still got her cell phone in her hand, and it's obvious she's not been paying attention to the grill guy like the rest of us. "My cat's gone."

"What?" I say.

Carly puts away her cell phone. "That was my mom. Marie ran away."

"Marie's her cat," Lizabett says to her brothers.

"Her expensive cat," Becca adds.

"Well, we'll have to find her," I say.

"Before next Thursday," Becca says.

That's right, I realize. Without the cat, Carly has no longer met her goal. Just when it is beginning to look as though I might reach my goal and make the Sisterhood completely successful with our goals, Carly loses hers.

"She can't have gone far," I say as I wind up my knitting. "We'll find her."

"Of course we will," Becca says as she walks over to the table and picks up her knitting to put in her backpack. "How far can a cat go at night?"

"Pretty far," Quinn says. "We'd better go with you. Firefighters are known for getting cats down from wherever they climb to."

"Good," Lizabett says with a smile.

I know what she's thinking. A walk in the dark should count as a date even if it's only to find a cat. The reason I know what she's thinking is that I'm thinking the same thing. I have a feeling Becca is thinking it, too. Maybe if I walk a little with each of Lizabett's brothers, that will count for three dates. Now, if we only get Carly's cat back tonight, we'll all be successful.

Chapter Four

Do not ask questions of fairy tales.
—Jewish proverb

I brought the fairy-tale quote to the Sisterhood shortly after we began to meet. During that time, I wanted nothing more than to have some "happilyever after" in my life. But there was none.

My dad was living in an apartment on California Avenue, and I kept waiting for him to move home where he belonged. I must have written his address down ten times in my journal, but I could never bring myself to go there and see him. I couldn't imagine just knocking on his door and saying "Hi, thought I'd drop by."

Added to that, my mom was still going to that church of hers, and I kept waiting for her to stop. It seemed as if I was waiting and waiting and nothing was happening the way I wanted it to happen.

You might have noticed that I have not ended the story of the Sisterhood even though I have already covered how we got started. I have always liked writing down my thoughts like this in a journal. I've had quite a few journals, but this is the first one that is devoted to telling about the Sisterhood, and I want to continue with it.

Earlier this evening, I asked the others if they were okay with me going on, since it is their story, too. It doesn't seem right to just end it with our sickness. I wanted to show who we are when we're well, too. Everyone said they wanted me to continue.

Becca even said she'd like to help.

I can tell Becca has something on her mind that she wants to add to the journal. She and I came back to The Pews after looking for

Carly's cat—which we did not find even though we looked every place we could in the darkness around Carly's house. I couldn't believe a mansion like that had something as ordinary as a cement foundation. But, even though we looked behind many bushes, we didn't see anything but that foundation. There was no cat.

Finally, everyone knew it was fruitless to continue tonight. We decided to talk in the morning and figure out what to do.

Lizabett and her brothers left from Carly's place, and Carly stayed home in case her cat returned on her own. Rose left earlier, as she works tomorrow and will have to drive all the way to Long Beach for her job. That left Becca and me to drive back to The Pews.

That's where we are now.

I keep finding reasons to put off giving Becca this journal. I'm not entirely sure what she wants to add, but I suspect it is something about me. She's been giving me a look all night that says I should be talking about the guys I've just met. But what's to say?

Forget that question. It's rhetorical. I'm sure Becca has plenty to say. I'm just not comfortable reading what others write about me. I guess I'll have to, though, if Becca puts her words right in the middle of the journal. Oh, well, here it goes.

Finally, she gives me the journal! Hi, this is Becca. I didn't think Marilee would ever turn over this book. She's right, of course. I do want to talk about her. But that's only because I don't think she will tell you everything herself. Have you ever had a friend like that?

You know what I mean then. You should have seen her when the grill guy came into the back room at the diner. She pretended not to notice him, but who could not notice him? Please. The man is drop-dead gorgeous. And with muscles—well, it made me shiver a little just looking at him, and he's never asked me out as he asked her out. There's got to be something still there, don't you think?

I thought so, too. And even if there's nothing from the past, there could be something in the future. I doubt Marilee's grill guy has to give a woman more than one long look with those eyes of his before the woman is falling all over him. Those eyes smolder—they remind me of some old movie star who I can't think of right now—maybe it's just that the eyes look as if they should belong to some movie star.

Anyway, the grill guy remembers Marilee. I could tell. She said he wouldn't, but I saw the way he looked at her. He remembers all right. If Carly weren't so upset about her cat, I would have suggested Marilee stay at The Pews while the rest of us went cat hunting. Lizabett's brothers all look as though they can find a cat if anyone can. But Marilee always calms Carly. I knew Marilee would want to be there for Carly—see, Marilee, I'm not writing bad stuff about you.

I did get a minute to talk to the grill guy before we left and I do have a few stats on him. Hey, somebody has to pay attention to business or none of us would meet our goals—you know what I'm saying? Anyway, the grill guy's restaurant is as good as home to half of the pro athletes in Los Angeles. He even takes phone messages for some of the guys. This Randy Parker, the grill guy, is a good catch. His diner must do more business than The Pews. Randy named some of the regulars who go to his place. Even I plan to go there and check it out some night.

Randy is also very nice. He told me he'll give me a free cup of coffee when I come to visit, and he'll introduce me to any players that might be around.

See how easy it would be for Marilee to connect up again with him? The guy is friendly.

But if I weren't here to tell you, I know Marilee wouldn't say a word. She isn't the most trusting person when it comes to men, and she finds it hard to believe that a good-looking guy like Randy would want to date her.

So, instead, she's going to tell you how pleasant Lizabett's brothers are. She'll say how they're sturdy and helpful. And that's all true. If there's a fire anyplace, they're the first ones I'd call. But trust me, none of them shine like the grill guy does.

That's all I wanted to say. And, Marilee, I want you to know that I wouldn't have had to say any of this if you were really writing down everything, including just how cute one particular guy is.

* * *

Well, I'm glad that's over. This is Marilee again. And, just for the record, it doesn't matter what I think about the grill guy. He's so far out of my league that there's no way he's going to ask me out. Besides, I turned him down six years ago. A guy doesn't forget a turndown—especially a guy like Randy. I can't believe any woman, except me, has ever been crazy enough to say no to him when he asked her out.

Fortunately, Becca and Carly both agreed I can count tonight as a date. Quinn MacDonald—you remember Lizabett's brother, "The Old Mother Hen"—even held my hand for a while. It wasn't totally romantic because he didn't hold my hand because he meant anything by it; he held it because he thought I was chilled. I knew he wasn't thinking romantic thoughts because he was fussing at me about the cold air, as if he was afraid I was going to have a relapse or something. He sounded like Rose.

I felt like telling Quinn that no one gets cancer from a slight chill, but I didn't want to give him a hard time. Besides, I figured a little hand-holding would make tonight count as a date for sure, and I owed the man for that.

Quinn was actually quite nice about the hand-holding.

He and I were searching behind Carly's house for the cat. Quinn had a flashlight, and he was aiming the light behind the shrubs. I must confess I was paying more attention to Carly's house than I was to finding her cat. I couldn't seriously believe any cat would run away from a house like this one.

The house—well, the mansion, really—was like something you would see on one of those television programs about the rich and famous. It was huge, and I counted six chandeliers just looking through the windows while searching for the cat. Carly's family even had a maid in a uniform who opened the door for Carly.

No wonder Carly doesn't talk about how she lives. Now that we all know, it will be hard not to feel jealous of her.

Quinn didn't seem rattled by the house, though. When I asked him about it, he just said there was a lot of wood in the house that was vulnerable to fire.

"And the roof must be in bad shape—a lot of these rain runoffs are clogged," Quinn said as he used a stick to poke one of the pipes that came almost to the ground. Decaying leaves came out the pipe.

"A cat would be too big to fit in those anyway," he said.

"Besides, it would go someplace warm," I added, just to show I was really worried about the cat and not just awestruck about the house. Between you and me, though, I figured even a fancy, purebred cat would be smart enough to come back to a house like this one.

Quinn nodded. "The grounds are so big, though, I doubt the cat's left the yard."

Quinn put down the stick he had and looked at me. That's when he took one of my hands to check it for chill. I think my comment about the cat going someplace warm tipped him off that I was cold. This time he frowned a little and rubbed my hands with his. "You should have mittens."

I shrugged. His hands were nice and warm. "I have pockets. I just need to put my hands in them."

Quinn smiled at that. "Before I know it,

you're going to call me an Old Mother Hen, too."

"Well, not quite." I noticed Quinn didn't let go of my hands even though he did stop rubbing them. It was okay with me that he kept holding my hands. It felt nice. Not be-still-my-heart romantic, but nice.

"Lizabett keeps saying I worry too much, but I can't help it. She was so sick," Quinn said.

"I know." For a minute I thought I still felt the chill even though my hands were warm by now. I had been most worried about Lizabett when we were all so sick. Maybe because she was the youngest, I wondered if she had the strength to fight anything.

"I wanted to do more, but all I could do was nag her about getting chilled or not eating her dinner or lifting a box when she knew I was right in the next room and could do it for her." Quinn's fingers curled around mine so that he wasn't just holding my hands to check for coldness anymore. I still wasn't sure he meant to be holding my hands, however. He just looked distracted—as if he was seeing what used to be.

I could sympathize with Quinn. My mom had wanted to do more to take care of me, too, but I fought it. When you're as sick as we had been in the Sisterhood, you want to stay as independent as you can for fear it will get even worse if you let down your guard.

"I'm sure Lizabett appreciates all you did," I said.

Quinn laughed at that.

He was right. I had to change what I had said. "Well, maybe she doesn't appreciate it yet, but someday she will. It's always good to have someone care about you when you're sick."

I decided it was time to give my mother another thank-you for all she'd done for me back then. I'd already thanked her a thousand times, but it still wasn't enough. Maybe I should give her some flowers. That would make her happy. I shut my mind to what would really please my mother the most because I had no intention of going to church with her.

"I wanted to be there for her," Quinn said. He was looking off into the dark night, and I wondered if he'd forgotten I was there even though he was still holding my hands. He was no longer smiling. "I promised my dad before he died that I'd do my best by the rest of the kids."

Quinn looked down at me when he'd finished talking, and I realized he'd never forgotten I was there. He was frowning a little bit as though he wanted to be sure I understood how important his promise had been.

"How old were you when your dad died?" I asked him.

"Nine."

I sucked in my breath. "No nine-year-old should have to make a promise like that."

"The others were even younger, and they were without a father, too. I wanted to step in where I could for them." Quinn smiled. "Even if one of them does call me an Old Mother Hen."

I have always been a soft touch for father stories. "I don't think you're an Old Mother Hen. I think what you've done for Lizabett is wonderful."

I knew even when I was talking to Quinn that I wished my dad had given me the kind of caring support, that Quinn had given to

Lizabett. I told myself that my dad tried to be supportive and maybe he did. He gave me the caps for my head. Granted, he never did actually talk to me about my cancer and how it was for me. I used to wonder if he knew how bad it was—as if maybe that Uncle Lou or my mother told him how it was when I was going through the worst of it. Anyway, if my dad knew how bad it got, he never said anything to me about it.

"The best part," I told Quinn as I looked up into his face, "is that you talked to Lizabett. Just having someone ask how you're doing—that's a good thing."

Quinn grunted. "Of course I talked to her. But I always wished I could have done something more than that."

We were silent for a minute, both of us remembering the years when Lizabett and I had been so sick. I couldn't look around me, so I kept my eyes on the ground. By now my hands were comfortable resting in Quinn's large palms. He has nice, strong hands.

"I bet your dad did lots of things for you," Quinn finally said.

I looked up at that. "No—well, he did

come to see me sometimes at the diner and bring me a cap for my hair."

Quinn was silent at that.

"My dad just isn't very good with emotional things," I added. I'd certainly had enough time while I was sick to think about my dad's responses to me, and that was what I had finally decided. And just because he wasn't very good with the emotional part of it didn't mean my dad didn't care about me. I wanted to believe that.

Still, the thought of it always brings me down a little, so I try not to dwell on it. Someday, I plan to ask my mother what she thinks about my dad and me, but so far I haven't brought the subject up and neither has she.

I didn't want to hold hands with Quinn any longer, so I slipped my hands out of his and put them in my pocket. The lining of my jacket was flannel, but it was still cold.

"What did your mother do?" Quinn asked quietly. "How did she handle your cancer?"

"She prayed a lot," I said.

I should have checked myself before I said that to Quinn. Even I could hear the bitterness in my voice. I didn't want to be that revealing about my feelings, especially not in front of someone I had just met.

"That's a bad thing?" Quinn asked cautiously.

I smiled nervously. "Of course not. Don't mind me. A lot of people pray about their troubles."

Quinn nodded. "But you wanted something else?"

"I wanted her to talk to me, not to God," I finally said.

Not that my mother didn't talk to me back then; it's just that she seemed to talk to God a whole lot more.

I sighed. Sometimes there's just no use pretending that I have my life all together.

Quinn was wearing a navy nylon jacket over his fireman's uniform. The nylon moved smoothly and felt good on my cheek when Quinn put his arm around me. "Maybe she needed to talk to God so she'd know what to say to you."

It was kind of nice to think that my mother had been taking steps to talk to me all that time she was praying. I'd never really thought of it that way. Instead, I'd always felt left out when she was praying, as if she and God were off by themselves doing the Christian thing and I was in another room by myself doing nothing.

I liked thinking I was part of the thing with my mother and God, and I was grateful Quinn had seen it that way so he could share it with me. It was nice. It was even nicer when Quinn drew me a little closer to himself, as well. For the first time, I could see why Lizabett called her brothers teddy bears.

After Quinn settled me next to him, he kept talking. "I know I used to pray up a storm to figure out what to do for Lizabett."

"My mom kept wanting me to go to church with her," I said.

Quinn chuckled. "Is that so bad? I go to church every Sunday, and I think it does me a world of good."

I was quiet at that one.

"You should come with me Sunday," Quinn said.

"Thanks, but—really, I couldn't—"

"It would count as a date," Quinn said softly and gave me a wink. "I figure one date tonight and one on Sunday. That only leaves us one more."

"You know?" I look up at him. I don't know why I had even held out hope that he didn't know.

It occurs to me all of a sudden that Lizabett has told Quinn a lot of things. Maybe all this talking back and forth isn't such a good thing after all.

"You know I could have picked an easy goal like getting a cat," I say in my own defense.

"I'm glad you didn't," Quinn says. "I'm hoping you'll have lunch with me on Sunday after church."

Well, what could I say? I'm thinking church counts as one date and the lunch afterward counts as another. As long as my mother doesn't know I've gone to church, it doesn't even need to mean anything in my life. If my mother knew, she'd renew her efforts to get me to go to church regularly; but if she doesn't know, everything will work out okay.

Quinn, Lizabett and their brothers left soon after Quinn invited me to church. Becca and I rode back to The Pews together in my car, but I didn't tell her about the final date with Quinn yet. She knew about tonight and the ball game on Saturday, but she didn't know about the third date on Sunday. I don't know why I didn't tell Becca exactly.

Maybe it was because the darkness along the roads was so restful. There aren't a lot of streetlights in San Marino, and it felt calm to be driving in that area. Also, I wanted to think about the dates a bit before I saw them chalked up on our board as fulfillment of my goal.

You know by now that Becca thinks the grill guy is the only man in the world, but I think there might be something to be said for a man like Quinn who worries about his little sister. I know most people worry about others who are sick with cancer. I guess it's natural.

After my hair loss, I had strangers come up to me and wish me well—which was kind of nice. But none of that made up for not hearing any words of concern from my own father. I had the baseball caps, but that was all. I used to wonder if my dad thought he was no longer my dad because he'd left my mother and me.

I don't mean to get too distracted here, I

just want to say that I think Quinn is a special brother. I'd put him up against the grill guy any day. It's not all about stormy eyes; sometimes it's about a man's heart, too.

Chapter Five

Being a princess isn't all it's cracked up to be.

—Princess Diana

Lizabett had already lost her hair when we started the Sisterhood, so I thought she would tell us that it was no big deal to go bald from the chemo. Instead, she grieved with each of us as though it was the final betrayal. In some ways, it was—there was no hope of hiding the cancer once the hair was gone.

Lizabett brought the princess quote to the Sisterhood after Carly, the last one to lose her hair, came in with a scarf tied around her head. Lizabett read us the quote and then handed us cardboard crowns to wear. We all took off our scarves, caps, and wigs. The crowns had shiny jewel-colored pieces of foil on them and someone had glued a band of felt around the bottom of each princess crown so the cardboard wouldn't rub against our bald heads.

Oh, we had fun that night. I couldn't remember the last time I had really laughed. You should have seen us with our bald heads and our crowns.

I didn't sleep well last night. I think that's what reminded me of the princess crowns. I didn't sleep well after wearing my crown, either. I wanted to savor the good feelings I'd had with the others that evening, and I was afraid if I slept, the feelings would be gone when I awoke.

I went to sleep last night knowing that this feeling that all was well for me would not last until the morning, either.

I have no doubt we will find Carly's cat. In fact, the cat is probably curled up in front of the massive door to Carly's house even as we speak, meowing for the maid to bring her breakfast on a silver tray. Once that happens—and Becca gets the acceptance letter she's expecting and Lizabett performs in her ballet—I will be the only one who will not have met my goal.

The solution of last night will not work in the cold light of morning today.

I know Quinn will see to it that I get my three dates if that's what I want. And that's nice of him. But I have to acknowledge that they're not *real* dates. He's just so used to taking care of Lizabett that his goodness overflows to me a little. I hate to meet my goal like that—with "pity dates."

The only thing for me to do is to actually get some real dates from a guy who doesn't feel obligated to ask me out. Of course, I don't know anyone who might be a prospect for a date like that unless Becca is right and the grill guy does remember me.

Actually, I hope he doesn't recall me too well. Maybe he will remember that he liked me enough to ask me out without remembering that I turned him down.

Yes, that would work.

I fluff up my hair and snip off a few rough edges before I pull out my old curling iron from the back of my closet. I'm not sure the iron will work, but the red light goes on, so it must. While I wait for the curling iron to heat, I put on some makeup—I actually found some eye shadow in a drawer by the bathroom sink.

It's ten o'clock in the morning when I get back to The Pews. That's my usual time to check in for work. Uncle Lou is the one who opens up the diner at six o'clock in the morning and handles the breakfast crowd.

I've always thought that Uncle Lou likes those four hours best of all the hours in the day because, at least in the first hour or so, he's alone in the diner and can remember the way things used to be. He plays old fifties music on the radio and I've noticed he puts the old salt and pepper shakers out for breakfast. He's muttered more than once that he's glad breakfast stays the same and hasn't gone all trendy on him. I haven't had the heart to tell him that some restaurants are adding cream cheese to their scrambled eggs and turkey sausage to their selections of meats.

Anyway, I have to park my car in a big, concrete parking structure a few blocks away from The Pews and walk to the diner. Since I have eyeliner on, I feel better about everything. It's a good morning for a walk. It is winter in Pasadena and the morning is bright and sunny. We get a lot of days like this in February. It's weather to make a person glad they are alive.

In the strong light of day like this, I feel ready for anything. On the way to the diner, I make my decision; I will find some real dates and let Quinn off the hook. Not that I won't still go to church with him, but I'll do that for a different reason.

As long as I'm doing things the right way, it's time I stopped being so superstitious about going to church. That's really what it is. I'm afraid that if I go to church once, Dad will somehow know and think I've gone over to Mom's side. And, if that doesn't happen, I'm nervous that Mom will know and start to hope I'll become a Christian.

But nothing will automatically happen just because I go to church. The roof will not cave in and the sky will not collapse.

There is no bad luck that will automatically come to me. Neither one of my parents will even know I've been to church unless I tell them. Besides, I can't live my life worrying about what my parents will think if I go to a religious service. I need to free myself of my fears.

I can smell bacon when I step into The Pews even though we stop serving breakfast at ten o'clock. I see Uncle Lou is leaning on the counter and talking with one of our regular customers.

"Good morning, Mr. Rushton." I nod to the man. Mr. Rushton is a retired schoolteacher and he eats breakfast here several times a week. He always orders the same thing—whole wheat toast with no butter and a bowl of oatmeal. I keep hoping Uncle Lou will take a hint or two from Mr. Rushton's diet, but I have a suspicion the bacon I smell frying is for Uncle Lou's midmorning snack since Mr. Rushton never eats fried meat.

I hang up my jacket on the hook behind the counter and reach for the coffeepot. I like to start my day with coffee.

"You're not wearing a cap." Uncle Lou

stops talking to Mr. Rushton and turns to me. "I never see you without a cap."

You would think I'd left my head off my shoulders instead of my cap off my head.

"And you've got makeup on," Uncle Lou continues as he steps a little closer to me and looks at me more carefully.

I shrug and reach for a cup for my coffee. "The Sisterhood thought it was time for me to get back to the regular way I look."

"You regularly wear a cap." Uncle Lou is looking at me as though he can't believe what he's seeing.

"Well, not before the—" I stop because I don't want to say *cancer* in front of Mr. Rushton. "Before my difficulties."

"But your father's coming by today," Uncle Lou finally says. "There's some baseball thing on television this afternoon, and he has the day off. And, he's bringing you a new cap. A special cap he ordered on eBay. From the New York Black Yankees—some all-black team that played in the late 1930s. He's all excited about it. The guys came out of Harlem and were some of the best ballplayers of their day. You don't find those caps everywhere."

My father has never brought me an historical cap before. He has given me caps from most of the current big-league teams, but there has never been a collectible cap. And him buying it on eBay—that's a first, too.

"You mean he bought a cap?"

"Of course. He buys all the caps," Uncle Lou looks surprised. "Nobody gives away those kind of caps anymore."

I always assumed my dad got the caps for free from his work. He works in the accounting department of a car dealership. I always thought the caps were leftover giveaways from sales days, and he just passed them on to me because he didn't want the caps himself.

"Oh." I swallow. I don't know why I always assumed Dad got the caps for free. I guess I never thought the caps meant that much to him, but were something that was just convenient for him to give me. I always pictured him grabbing one from a big bin on his way out of the office on the nights he planned to stop by the diner. "I have some of the caps in my office. I'll go put one on."

Uncle Lou nods. "Your dad likes to see you wearing the caps he's given you."

I nod. I don't know what to say. Fortunately, Mr. Rushton stands up, so I smile at him as I reach out to pick up his plate. "Have a good day."

As I take hold of the plate, Mr. Rushton pats my hand and says, "You're a good girl. Your dad must be proud."

Uncle Lou takes a deep breath. "Of course he is. We're all proud of our Marilee."

"I am very fortunate," I say as I wait for Mr. Rushton to give Uncle Lou and me another nod as he walks to the door.

The truth is that I know I am fortunate. Things could be so much worse for me. I'm cancer free. I am a part-owner of a business I love. Uncle Lou is great to me. My mom is there any time I need to lean on her. And my dad—who knew he was actually buying me the caps?

It doesn't take long for Uncle Lou to get back behind the counter and start getting ready for the lunch crowd. I slip back to my office and find a baseball cap to wear for the day. I haven't worn the Boston Red Sox one for a while. As long as I'm back in my office, I decide to check my messages. Carly sent an e-mail this morning to the Sisterhood that her cat is still missing. Then she asks if we'll help look some more for the cat later today.

After I read her e-mail, I realize this is the first time I have ever heard Carly ask for help. So I call her on her cell phone.

Carly answers, and I can tell she's been crying. I've never heard Carly cry. She went through all her chemo without shedding a tear as far as I know. I've got to tell you, the sound of Carly crying alarms me.

"You didn't find—" I can't ask Carly if she's found her cat's body. That'll make her cry even more. "I mean, do you have more news on your cat?"

Carly takes a tearful breath. "No."

"I can come over to your place right now if you want me to," I say. Uncle Lou will understand if I need to leave for a little while.

Now I can really hear Carly crying.

"No, don't come here," Carly says. "But can I come there?"

"Of course."

"I'll be right there," Carly says, and we hang up.

Okay, now I am over-the-top worried. I

have been assuming that Carly's cat would have already realized she was hungry and turned her nose toward the kitchen. I know Carly is worried about her cat, but I had no idea she is this worried.

Carly lives about ten minutes away from The Pews, and it will take her an additional five minutes to park and come inside. I give Lizabett and Becca both a call, leaving messages for both of them on their cell phones that they should call me since we need to find Carly's cat.

I'm glad I have my baseball cap on again as I walk out of my office. Those caps give me some measure of comfort, and I may wear one for the rest of my life on the days when I am worried.

The smell of bacon is still there when I step into the main part of The Pews. I hear voices in the kitchen, but there are no customers at the moment. It's usually quiet in the middle of the morning like this, so Uncle Lou will be fine if I go back with Carly and spend some time looking for her cat.

I figure one of the delivery guys is in the kitchen, and I give Uncle Lou a minute to finish with him before I go in. I'm afraid my worry shows on my face, and I don't want to alarm anyone, especially not some guy who is just delivering the bread order. I start refilling napkin dispensers for something to do with my hands. The dispensers are still almost full.

I must admit, I am surprised about Carly and her cat. I assumed she wanted this cat because the cat had that history with Marie Antoinette. If that was the case, though, Carly wouldn't be this upset. I mean, let's face it, the cat might be cold and hungry, but it's probably all right. It's not time to panic yet.

I finish up with the napkin dispensers and look around for something else to do to keep my mind busy. Uncle Lou is still talking to whoever is in the kitchen. Carly must be on her way over here by now.

It all worries me. You probably know what I am thinking. Every time someone in the Sisterhood gets more upset than we'd expect, the rest of always ask the same question: Did she get a bad test result that she hasn't told us about? I think Carly would tell us if something was wrong, but I'm not sure.

I line up the sugar packets in their container so they are straight.

Even though everyone in the Sisterhood has been cancer free for almost six years now, we are not sure we will stay that way. Of course, no one anywhere is sure. Cancer tends to come or recur whether it's expected or not. We are just more aware than most people of the way our bodies can turn on us.

I hear Uncle Lou's voice growing louder and look up to see him and Randy Parker walk through the kitchen door and back into the main part of the diner where I am standing making the sugar packets orderly.

I don't know what the grill guy is doing here, but he couldn't have picked a worse time to come and talk with Uncle Lou.

I have my eyeliner and lipstick on, but with the baseball cap hanging over my face, I'm sure none of my new makeup shows. I would take the cap off, but my hair tends to fly in every direction when I do that, so I just push the brim up so that, hopefully, my newly made-up face shows. Maybe I'll look sporty cute.

"You're here," Uncle Lou says, sounding

happy to see me. "I was just telling Randy you could give him a tour of the place—get him reacquainted."

The day is nice and bright, and sun is shining in through the diner's open blinds.

I can see the grill guy, and he is looking friendly. Becca is right. The guy has a nice smile, and he doesn't seem to be aware that he's at the top of the list when it comes to looks.

"I'd be happy to show you around, but I can't right now." I look at Randy. My timing just isn't good with this guy. "A good friend of mine is coming here any minute, and I need to talk to her first." That doesn't sound adequate. I don't want to blow the grill guy off twice even if he probably doesn't remember the last time I turned down an opportunity to be with him. "It's Carly—she lost her cat."

"Oh," Randy says sympathetically. With the sunlight shining on him, I can see where Randy's face has filled out in the six years since he used to work here. He's got that movie-star jaw now.

"It's a rare cat," I add out of nervousness. "It cost two thousand dollars."

I wince. I shouldn't mention the price tag.

"Of course, Carly is very fond of her cat, so it's not about the money."

Randy whistles. "Must be some cat for two thousand dollars."

I am saved from rattling off at the mouth any further by the sound of the door opening.

It's Carly. Her eyes are puffy, and her hair isn't in its usual state of perfection. I can tell she hasn't noticed the grill guy or Uncle Lou. All she sees is me.

My heart sinks as I open my arms. Something is really wrong.

"I'm an awful cat owner," Carly wails as she lets me give her a hug.

I breathe a sigh of relief. It's not her health.

"Cats run away sometimes," I say as I pat Carly's shoulder. "Well, and sometimes they don't even run away—they just get curious and walk over to that bush, and then another bush and before you know it, they can't find their way back. Your cat probably didn't mean to leave. And she can't have gone far."

"Unless someone took her," Randy adds.

Carly stiffens when she realizes someone is in the diner besides her and me and Uncle Lou. She pulls back.

"I'm sorry," Carly wipes her eyes and stands a little farther away from me. "I didn't know you had company."

"This is Randy—you remember, he's going to fill in for Uncle Lou on the grill," I say, even though I know very well that Carly knows who Randy is. I wouldn't want him to think that all of my friends know who he is, though—well, you know.

"And don't be sorry," Randy says as he takes a step closer to Carly. "I know what it's like to lose a pet."

I can't imagine the grill guy crying over anything, but he sounds as if he knows how Carly feels.

"Do you really think someone could have stolen Marie? That's my cat's name." Carly explains to the grill guy as she sits down at one of the tables. "I never thought of that. Maybe someone's holding her for ransom."

I'm glad I told Randy how valuable the cat is, so he won't think Carly is crazy. I've never heard of anyone holding a cat for ransom before, but if the cat is worth two thousand dollars, it might happen.

Randy sits down at the table with Carly

and takes her hand and pats it. "If someone is holding it for ransom, they'll let you know soon."

"I can't stand the waiting."

I don't think Carly knows I'm here any longer. She's just looking at my grill guy as though he has all the answers in the world. I'm not sure how I feel about that. I mean, I never actually had a date with the grill guy, but I'd be lying if I said he wasn't somebody in my life—well, maybe not the actual person Randy Parker, but my remembered, longed-for grill guy is somebody.

You know, it's strange. There are four of us in the Sisterhood—five, if you count Rose—but we have never had a problem before with any two of us being interested in the same man. We even go for different movie stars. Becca goes for the crazy action guys like Tom Cruise. Carly goes for the old movie stars like Rock Hudson. Lizabett goes for musicians—especially classical musicians. She likes the easy flowing nature of classical music, and that's probably why she likes ballet, too.

Me—I go more for the costars than the

stars. Don't ask me why. I'll find some obscure guy in a movie and dream about him, even though, when I mention him to other people, no one remembers him in the movie.

I look over at Randy and Carly. He's still patting her hand, but she's stopped looking as though she's going to cry. I can't see Randy taking an obscure role in any movie. Maybe he *is* more Carly's type.

"We could ask," I hear Carly say because she's lifted her head and is looking at Uncle Lou.

I think I've lost a little bit of the conversation.

"Carly mentioned that her cat seemed to like the smell of bacon in the morning," Randy says to Uncle Lou. "So, I thought maybe if we put some bacon on the sidewalk around her house, we could draw the cat out from where it's hiding."

"That's a great idea," I say. I do a check on my emotions the way Rose taught us all to do and, to be honest, I don't find that—once I give it a minute to settle—I'm really troubled about what is happening here between Carly and Randy.

Is that good or bad? I don't know. Maybe it's just the shock of it all—you know how they say you can't feel a gunshot wound right away because your body is in shock. Maybe I'm like that. Nice and cool now, but in a few minutes or hours, I'll be doubled-over in pain. I've dreamed about the grill guy for years.

What will it be like if Carly and Randy start dating?

Becca will be upset. That much I know. She's counting on the grill guy to ask me out a few times so I can meet my goal.

I give the grill guy another look. Maybe the shock is wearing off a little, because I'm starting to feel sad that I won't have him to date. He honestly seems like a nice guy. You should see him now. He's holding Carly's hand, and his mind is still on bacon—and paper towels. He's decided the bacon needs to be wrapped in paper towels so it doesn't get the sidewalk all greasy. I don't know many guys who could hold the hand of a beautiful blonde like Carly and be thinking about bacon grease. He seems like a real decent sort of person. Maybe I shouldn't be so quick to give up on him.

Chapter Six

A camel makes an elephant feel like a jet plane.

—Jackie Kennedy

You would think Carly would be the one to bring this quote to the Sisterhood because Jackie O is as close to a queen as this country has every had. But it wasn't Carly who brought it—it was Rose. We spent most of our time that night trying to figure out what the quote meant, and I think that's why Rose brought it to us. Rose always seemed to know when we'd spent enough time sharing our troubles and needed to have something else to think about.

"It just means everything is relative," Becca said. She didn't like quotes that were ambiguous.

"I think it means it pays to fly first-class," Carly said. The rest of us were silent a moment, trying to imagine what it would be like to do anything first-class.

"I think Mrs. Kennedy just said it to make the elephant feel better," Lizabett said. "Like when everyone is complaining about someone, and they all just need to take a minute to think about what the person could be doing that might even be worse than what they're doing."

Some days I need to be reminded that each of us in the Sisterhood see things in our own ways. It's hard to remember that my friends are different than I am and have as many opinions as I do. Now that I'm writing the journal for all of us, it's important that I realize that I can't really speak for everyone.

I am particularly reminded of that because Carly has just asked me if she can make a few remarks in the journal while Uncle Lou fries up the bacon so we—she, Randy, and I—

can go over to her house and try to coax her cat home with the smell.

I, of course, said yes to Carly when she asked to make some comments. As I said earlier, this is not my personal journal. It's *our* journal. Carly's entitled to give her opinion in it. I'm going to fold the journal to a new page before I give it to Carly, though. I don't want her to read what I just wrote a few pages ago about her and Randy—at least not right now.

I'm going to tell you something else, too. It's strange, but Carly, even with all of her beauty, doesn't necessarily have a lot of confidence with men. I've never understood that, but I know she deserves a nice guy who will see her as more than a beautiful woman. If she and Randy get together, I'll try to be happy for them. Well, I'm folding here.

Hi, this is Carly. I know Marilee is telling you all about what's happening, but I think I should explain about my cat. I know better than to fall apart over a cat. My mother taught me restraint from the first day my parents and I moved in with my uncle and his wife in San Marino.

My mother has impressed upon me that we are guests in her brother's home and should do nothing to bring dishonor to his name or unpleasantness to his household. The unspoken message is that, with my father's alcoholism, we have already brought enough shame with us. We owe my uncle for permitting us to move in with him and my aunt. Not many men would be so generous.

Because of this, my mother never allowed me to have any pets, even before I developed allergies, or visits from friends while I was growing up. She only reluctantly allowed the coming and going that came with the nurse's visits when I had cancer.

I should say here that my mother is right. We *are* guests, and we shouldn't abuse my uncle's hospitality. My mother was injured in a car accident years ago and isn't strong enough to work. My father's drinking has gotten him fired from so many jobs, no one will hire him anymore. I don't know what would have happened to us if it were not for my uncle's willingness to support us. If I sound frustrated, it's only because it has been a lonely life.

Of course, I know I should be grateful, and I try to be. After all, how many young girls have their own suite of rooms—bedroom, bathroom and playroom?

Lizabett has complained there wasn't enough room in their house before she moved out. Even Marilee and her mother live in a small duplex. I suspect that is why both Marilee and Lizabett are fascinated with my uncle's house. It's the bigness of it all.

I may as well give you the statistics so you can decide if you are impressed, too. The house was built in 1905 and completely gutted and remodeled when my uncle bought it in 1976. The place is always on the garden tour the women's club gives to raise money. My aunt loves showing off her house. For a whole month of Sundays, we have plastic runners all over the carpet and huge floral bouquets in each room.

Of course, my suite and my parents' suite, plus the closet that was remodeled to be a galley kitchen for us, are never on the tour. We always try to keep to our rooms anyway, so, except for walking in at night and out in the morning, we never even see the plastic runners for the tours.

It's a three-floor house, not counting the attic, with forty-five hundred feet on each floor.

The main floor has a master bedroom suite in addition to three living rooms, a huge dining room and a kitchen. The cook has a bedroom and bathroom for her use behind the kitchen.

The second floor is mostly suites of bedrooms—there are seven total suites each with a bedroom, bathroom and second room. The suites used by my parents and me are at the opposite end of the house from the rooms used when my aunt and uncle have guests. We seldom take our meals with my uncle and aunt at any time, but we definitely do not when they have guests.

There is an elevator that goes to the big ballroom on the third floor and stairs that go to attic bedrooms that house the servants, in addition to the cook, that my uncle employs—currently, a housekeeper and a gardener.

I was in awe of the house when I first saw it, so I can understand how Marilee and Lizabett feel. The house is tucked back off the street with trees that, when they are fully leafed out, almost hide it from any cars that drive by. In the summer, if my aunt and uncle are gone for the day, I lie down in the trees and pretend I'm in a forest. I love days like that.

In the back of the house there is a pool and a tennis court. On hot summer days, I used to wish my aunt and uncle would go on vacation so my mother would let me use the pool. She would only let me use the pool if they were out of town for several days, because she did not want them to come back and see me in their pool. After all, it was, she reminded me, their pool.

Fortunately, the house is cool in the summer.

All year round the inside of the house shines. The floors are always buffed and the crystal is always dusted and placed where it catches the light of the sun.

It is the housekeeper, Susan, who likes the reflection from the crystal to shine on all of the walls. I swear no one but her and I even notice it. I only see the main part of the house occasionally, but Susan says I am the only one who ever comments on how pleasant she makes the house look. If my aunt notices, she never says anything.

Anyway, being allowed to have a cat in my rooms is a big concession. My mother had to ask my uncle if it was all right—and he is not the easiest person to get an appointment with. The only reason my mother did it is because she is afraid I am thinking of moving out of my uncle's house.

She is right to worry. One of the reasons I wanted my cat, Marie, is so that I would have someone to be with me when I get a place of my own. Of course, to do that I also need to find a job. I have several applications out, but I am not saying anything until I hear something back.

I know I have rambled, but I hope you can understand why Marie is so important to me. Besides, she is the only living thing who has ever depended on me, and I don't want to let her down.

I keep picturing what her feline ancestors must have felt like when Marie Antoinette didn't come for them. I wonder if Marie Antoinette had left money to pay for the cats' keep, because, if so, the money must have eventually run out. Did someone then reluctantly take care of the cats out of duty like my uncle is taking care of my parents and me? It's not easy to always be beholden to someone. But what else would they do? They were royal cats. Would they even know how to take care of themselves in the wild?

I know my cat, Marie, is not exactly royal, but she won't know how to take care of herself either. Randy says I should try not to worry until we find her.

Oh, before I end this, I want to add that Randy is a really nice guy. Marilee is a lucky girl. I'm sure the reason he came back to The Pews this morning is because he wanted to see Marilee again. I know I shouldn't take him away from her to look for my cat, but I'm glad he's willing to help me. Maybe he and Marilee will hunt behind some trees today. I saw Quinn holding her hand last night, and I figure if the bushes can make a practical man like Quinn turn romantic, then the trees will make Randy ask Marilee out on a date. Wouldn't that be nice?

It's me again, Marilee. Carly folded her pages back, too, but she told me she wrote about her cat. She said I can read what she wrote later, but not right now. We've got things to do. I'm glad the cat is what's on her mind.

Of course, the whole diner smells like bacon now.

My uncle and Randy have just fried up five pounds of bacon, and I'm thinking we'll have every cat in the neighborhood at Carly's place if we leave all those paper-wrapped packets of bacon on the streets near her house.

I got a call from Becca, and she said she needed to make some phone calls before she could drive out to begin the search for Carly's cat again. I also got a message from Lizabett, who said she had to go to an emergency meeting at her ballet studio and that The Old Mother Hen was taking her because he had something to do in this area and would bring her over to Carly's place as soon as the meeting was over.

You'll notice my handwriting is a little squiggly here since I'm writing this in the backseat of Randy's Jeep while he's driving us over to Carly's place. I figure that will give Carly and Randy a little privacy in the front seat. Good plan, huh?

I was surprised at the Jeep. It's a decent Jeep, but not the latest model. It's white and it looks as though it rides best with the windows down and the radio cranked up—it's the stripped-down model with no cassette or CD player. Fortunately for me it does have a backseat. Randy didn't strike me as the Jeep kind of a guy. I had him pegged for an Acura or a small BMW. I know Carly's definitely not the Jeep kind, so I don't know how they'll work that out.

I can't hear what they've been saying in the front seat, so I don't know how it is going with them. I was ready for the wind because I had my cap on my head and my hair is short anyway, but Carly, with her long blond hair, is looking as though she's faced down a tornado.

Carly is too polite to complain, however. Either that or her cat really is all that is on her mind.

Randy drives us right up to the house where Carly lives and stops the engine.

"Maybe you should check first and be sure no one has seen your cat around before we go out looking," Randy says to Carly as he gets out of his door and goes around to open the car door for her.

I don't know many guys who open a woman's car door, but it's the kind of gesture that seems natural in these surroundings and I don't want to be gauche, so I decide to wait a minute before I just swing my own door open. Besides, I'm still writing.

Of course, I have two arms and have been opening doors for myself for years, so when Carly starts to walk up the sidewalk and Randy turns to follow her, I take that as my cue to put down my journal and open the door myself.

I won't have time to write in the journal for a few minutes while we put the bacon packets all along the drive and in front of Carly's house, but I'll let you know how the bacon works. As I said before, we're bound to attract any animal around.

The nice policeman let me go get my journal so I'll have something to do while I wait for him to write up his report. Carly and Randy are just sitting at the side of the curb talking to each other, looking like stylish refugees, so I thought I'd give them some time alone and bring you up-to-date at the same time. I don't know whether to start with the good news or the bad news.

The good news is that Carly saw her cat. We'd put bacon packets all along the street near the house and along most of the drive up to the house when Carly saw her cat come up to sniff one of the packets. The cat was outside the yard of Carly's house, but very close by. The bad news is that, before we could get to the cat, the police siren scared the cat up some different trees, and we haven't seen her since.

Of course, the really bad news is that leaving pieces of fried bacon wrapped in paper towels along the streets of San Marino is considered littering rather than cat trapping. We tried to explain our strategy to the police officer, but all we succeeded in doing was attracting a collection of neighbors who are now all standing around while the police officer is giving us our littering tickets.

Some of the neighbors don't think we should be given tickets, mostly, it appears, because we are young people, and young people just do silly things like this. Others of the neighbors think we should be given stiff penalties because we are young people and need to learn a lesson here because it might turn us away from a life of crime later. No one seems willing to debate whether the bacon incident really constitutes a crime.

I'm sitting in the passenger seat of the police car so I have a ringside seat for the debate. I don't know what people think I am doing as I write away in my journal, but I see one of the neighbors give me a nervous look.

"You said it's bacon, right?" that neighbor asks the policeman.

"Yes, sir," the policeman says.

"You checked all of the packets?" the man continues.

The policeman looks up from his notebook at this. "No, why?"

"Well, didn't it occur to you that it could be a bomb or a biological substance or anthrax or something?"

I hear several gasps.

"You mean terrorism?" a woman shrieks. "Here in San Marino?"

"We don't have things like that here," another woman says.

"But we could," the man persists. "A lot of important people live here. Scientists for the Jet Propulsion Laboratory. Professors from Cal Tech. An incident here would get the press right away."

"There is no incident," the policeman says.

I wish that the policeman's voice sounded more confident, but it doesn't. He's looking at the other packets that are still sitting on the street. I don't know what to do now. I glance over at Carly and Randy, and they are so engrossed in some conversation they're having that they don't realize the mob around us has turned ugly. I keep writing because I don't want to call out to Carly and Randy. I'm worried if I do, someone will think I'm starting a riot.

"Maybe I should call for a HazMat team to clean up those other packets, though," the policeman says as he reaches for the communications piece in his car.

I slouch a little farther down in the passenger seat of the car as the policeman sits down and makes his call, telling the dispatcher that there is a possible contaminant on the streets of San Marino.

The only good thing is that the policeman has stopped writing the littering ticket. I haven't even had the nerve to ask him yet what the fine will be for littering. I'd guess it will be a hundred dollars at least. There goes my piggy bank.

I stop writing for a few minutes because I don't want the policeman to think I'm writing down any scientific formulas for anthrax or anything, but the neighbors are starting to go back to their homes. Before long, the policeman leaves the car and goes down to talk to Carly and Randy. I start writing again just as I hear what sounds like a dozen police sirens coming this way. One thing about littering in San Marino—it's not a quiet crime.

Of course, by now, the maid and cook at Carly's house are out on the front porch watching the drama. They're both wearing black-and-white uniforms. I wonder how they feel about being so obviously identified as servants.

The cop cars are all here now. I slouch a little farther down in the police car where I am. I want them to know I am already arrested. They are a fierce-looking bunch.

No sooner do the cop cars get here than a silver blue Ford Taurus pulls up next to the lead police car. Quinn MacDonald, in full fireman uniform, steps out. I've never been so happy to see a man in my life. If anyone can handle a dozen policemen, it is The Old Mother Hen. He'll help us.

I can't hear what Quinn is saying to the police officers, but I can see that they're listening to him. For all I know, he's saying Carly, Randy and I are insane and need padded cells. I hope that's not what he is saying, because the policemen are nodding.

A van drives beside the police car where I am sitting, and more men pile out. This time the men have a camera, and I take a closer look at the van. It is the *Pasadena Star* news team. Maybe you won't have to read the journal here to find out what happens next, after all. The news team has a microphone angled toward the policeman who first picked us up for littering.

I hear a tap at my window and look up to see Quinn MacDonald motioning me to come out of the police car. Fortunately, the policemen never locked me in the car, so I guess its okay to step outside.

"Are you all right?" Quinn says when I stand up.

I nod, but he pulls me into his arms anyway. I feel safer than I did when I was inside the policeman's car. Quinn's chest is solid, and I can hear his heartbeat.

"He's giving us a ticket," I say to Quinn's shoulder. I'm not really complaining by now.

"You're lucky he's not aiming his gun at you," Quinn says. "Suspicions grow quickly these days."

"It's only bacon," I say as I pull away so I can see Quinn's face.

"I know," Quinn says with a flash of a smile. "I had to go pick up a packet and eat it before they believed it was safe. It was good, too—even cold. I didn't have breakfast."

"Uncle Lou swears his grill fries the best bacon in all of Los Angeles County," I say.

"I believe him," Quinn says.

Now that Quinn isn't hugging me, it feels a little strange that he's still holding me in his arms. There's definitely a difference between a hug and some holding.

"You're welcome to come by and have a real breakfast some morning," I say. "On the house."

"I'll do that," Quinn says, and he dips his head and lightly kisses me.

Oh.

I can't help but wonder if a kiss is always a kiss. With Quinn a kiss could be just a way to soothe a hurt place. I mean, he knew I had a stressful time with the police and all. Was he just giving me a comforting kiss?

I honestly don't know. Anyway, the kiss seemed the end of it. Once he'd kissed me, he stepped away.

The kiss was so quick I don't think anyone else saw it. All in all, I decide the best thing to do with a kiss like that is to forget it ever happened. My mind is rattled enough without adding a kiss to it. I can't even think of what Quinn is doing here until I remember Lizabett.

Lizabett is over talking to Carly and Randy. Lizabett looks worried, so they probably told her that Carly's cat has climbed back up into these trees. I look up into the trees myself. Of course, I don't see a cat. A clawed animal would have a hundred places to hide in the trees around here. Not that that will stop us. We need to find Carly's cat.

Chapter Seven

It's the friends you can call up at 4 a.m. that matter.

—Marlene Dietrich

I never knew what friendship was until I had cancer. Rose was the one who brought this quote to us several months after we began the Sisterhood. We all knew we could call Rose whenever we needed to talk to her, but that night we made a pact that, if we needed to talk to someone, we could call on each other no matter what time of night or day it was. I didn't think it would make such a difference, but it did. From that night on, we were more than friends—we were sisters. Long live the Sisterhood of the Dropped Stitches!

I can see Lizabett has been crying even though she isn't crying right now. She and I are standing beside Quinn's car waiting for him to finish talking to the policeman. It's getting close to noon, and the sun is shining down upon us. Of course, it's February, so it's not hot. Even at that, though, all of us are too aware of skin cancer to want to be out in the direct sun for long.

"He's telling the police what that cat means to Carly," Lizabett says after a moment. She looks over to the trees where Carly's cat is hiding. "About us making our goals and all."

Lizabett doesn't sound annoyed with Quinn, which makes me wonder even more what is wrong. She's always annoyed if Quinn speaks on anyone else's behalf.

"We'll get the cat down before next Thursday," I say, figuring Lizabett is worried about everyone meeting their goals. Carly and Randy are by those trees now, calling up to the cat. "Marie's going to be really hungry soon, and is going to jump down into Carly's arms.

I'm even planning to have my three dates done by Thursday so we'll all meet the deadline."

Lizabett takes a hiccup of a breath. "Then it'll only be me that's holding everyone back."

Ah, so that's what the problem is. "Don't worry. Everyone gets nervous before they perform. You might be scared now, but you'll do fine in the ballet. You've practiced and you're ready for it. You'll want to dance when Wednesday comes around."

Lizabett looks away from me and focuses on the sky to her right. There's nothing there but a few clouds. "It won't matter if I want to dance or not. There's not going to be a performance. It's the theater."

"What? I thought everything was set." I have never been to the old theater where Lizabett's performance is to be held and, as far as I know, there are no other productions of anything scheduled there. As I said before, I don't think the old theater has been used at all for the past few years and it is lucky to have the ballet scheduled there. They must have gotten a better offer, though. "I can't believe the theater is bumping your ballet."

"They're not bumping us," Lizabett says. "The fire department closed them down today."

"Oh."

Lizabett still hasn't turned to look at me, so I just stand here patiently. I know there's something more.

"I think Quinn is the one who told them to close the place," Lizabett finally whispers.

"Oh, he wouldn't—" I stop myself. Would he? All of Lizabett's brothers work for the fire department. Quinn would certainly have the connections to do something like that. I hate to think he would, though.

"He's probably worried I'll fall on my leg where I had surgery," Lizabett says softly. Her voice is flat and defeated. "I suppose he means well."

I look over at Quinn. He is still talking to the policeman, although they have obviously finished with business and are now just laughing and socializing. "I can't believe he'd stop your ballet."

I say the words because I can't believe anyone would stop their younger sister from performing. "I mean, if he did close the place down, it's because there *is* a fire hazard and not because he just doesn't want you to do your ballet."

"He never thought I was strong enough for the ballet moves," Lizabett says as she shrugs her shoulders. "And, with the cancer I had in my leg—he worries."

I look over at Quinn again. Is there such a thing as too much protection?

"Have you asked him?" I finally say to Lizabett. "You need to ask him."

Lizabett nods, but her face looks as drained as it used to when she was fighting cancer. "I suppose so."

I don't have anything else to offer her for comfort, so I open the door to Quinn's car and pick up the journal I had set there. "You can write in the Sisterhood journal for a while if you want."

"Really?" Lizabett says. Her eyes look happier. "I thought you were the only one writing in it."

"Both Becca and Carly have written something—you should, too."

Lizabett takes the journal from me. "What did they write about?"

"Becca wrote about the grill guy and Carly

wrote about her cat. At least she *said* she was writing about her cat—she turned her pages down and told me it's private. She'll let me know when it's okay to read the pages."

"I'm going to write about The Old Mother Hen," Lizabett says as she opens the back door to Quinn's car. "And I think I'll fold my pages, too."

I nod. "Fair enough."

Hi, this is Lizabett. You already know what The Old Mother Hen did, so I'm just going to tell you that I wish I'd never introduced him to the Sisterhood. Do you know how hard it is to have a life when you have an older brother watching your every step? What The Old Mother Hen needs is a life of his own—which he'll never have as long as he keeps worrying about me.

I am taking a minute to look up from the journal, and I've got to tell you what I see. Marilee has walked over to stand beside Quinn, and my big brother has stepped back a bit so there is room for him and Marilee to stand side by side while they continue talking to the policeman.

I close my eyes when I see the two of them and say a prayer. Quinn has been teaching me about prayer, and I'm trying to make it more a part of my daily life—I wonder what he'd think of this prayer, though. When I open my eyes, guess what I see? Quinn has put his arm around Marilee. Thank you, God.

Isn't that great? I don't know why I didn't think of this before. The best way to get Quinn to stop worrying about me is to give him someone else to worry about, someone like a girlfriend—maybe even a wife.

Imagine how much freedom I would have if Quinn were married. And, if he had children, I'd never have to worry again. He wouldn't have time to close down theaters or to buy me extra vitamins.

I stop writing to think a minute. Quinn has never let himself get too serious about any of his girlfriends. I suppose it's because he feels so obligated to take care of me and my other brothers. It might not be so easy for me to get him married off. I can see he likes Marilee, though.

Wait a minute. While I'm sitting here

looking at Quinn and Marilee, I see the grill guy walk over to them.

If I'm going to get Quinn and Marilee together, I'm going to have to work fast, before the grill guy decides to ask Marilee out again. I'm not sure how much of a chance Quinn would have if the choice were between him and this grill guy. Don't get me wrong. I love my brother. And he's handsome in a sturdy sort of a way. But the grill guy is, well—whooee. Let's just say Quinn would have a better chance without the competition of a guy like that.

Oh, Marilee is walking back here, so I'm going to finish this up and fold back the pages. And, Marilee, if you unfold those pages before I say you can—you deserve to hear yourself written about. I have a hair clip in my pocket and I'm going to put that on the pages once I've folded them just to remind you that this here is private.

Hi, this is Marilee again. I'm sitting in my office for a minute. I just had a sandwich, and I'm going to bring you up-to-date. Things have been spinning. Quinn drove Lizabett and me back to The Pews. Randy and Carly were going to come, but Lizabett thought she'd caught a glimpse of Carly's cat and insisted that the cat must be waiting for everyone to leave before it came down from its perch in the trees. Carly urged Randy to come back with us in Quinn's car, but Lizabett said someone needed to stay with Carly and Randy was the tallest one, so he'd be a good one to stay.

I thought that was odd, because even if he is tall, Randy couldn't reach up to the branches in those trees. No one could. But no one else seemed troubled by that fact. Randy didn't object—neither did Carly. So Quinn, Lizabett and I came back together.

I found it a tense ride. Lizabett is obviously angrier with Quinn than I had thought. She absolutely refused to ride in the front seat with him. She even opened the trunk and found an old black scarf that she tied around her head, warning us that she wouldn't be able to hear with the scarf but she needed to wear it anyway because she felt as if she had a bit of an earache coming on.

I, of course, didn't want to bring up the

topic of the theater that had been closed, so I was prepared to chatter away about the weather or some other benign topic. I was surprised when Quinn asked me what kind of books I liked to read and if I had any places I wanted to visit if I could travel.

I remember once in high school I had accepted a date with this guy in my class because I thought he was a reader. As it turned out, he was just carrying around this library book that he'd checked out two years ago. He liked to have it with him because it was heavy and he used it to prop open the door to his locker. When I asked him about the library fine—I mean, he would have racked up quite a fine—he looked at me like he'd never heard of such a thing and said he didn't read his mail anyway.

My point is that at least Quinn has read some books.

I don't know what to do about Quinn. I got carried away when I found out he liked some of my favorite books and I sort of invited him to come back this afternoon and watch the baseball retrospective with my dad and me.

I hope he doesn't come. I never should

have invited him. My relationship with my dad isn't the smoothest thing in my life, and I'm not sure it's something someone else should witness—at least not someone who doesn't know me very well yet.

I become quiet around my dad. Oh, we yell like anything at the television when some referee makes a call that we don't like, and I have no problem hollering when our team makes a point. But none of that is really *talking.* I don't do very well at the talking part. It's almost painful.

And now Quinn will be there to see how withdrawn I can be.

Oh, well, like I said—maybe Quinn won't come. After all, he's already used up most of his day off, and, it wasn't a complete day off because he gave a speech to some schoolkids this morning before he and Lizabett stopped at Carly's. Once he drives Lizabett home, he probably won't want to come back, even though he said he would.

And, there's always the possibility that Lizabett will get up enough nerve to ask him if he deliberately tried to ruin the ballet production so she couldn't dance. If he needs to talk to her, that would certainly keep him away.

Yes, there is any number of things that could keep the afternoon from being a disaster, so I'm just going to put my cap on my head and go meet my fate.

Uncle Lou is in the room where we have the big-screen television, and he looks up when I walk in. Business is good this afternoon, but everyone is just having something to eat in the main part of The Pews. No one else is in the television room.

Uncle Lou nods his approval at the cap I am wearing, and I can't help but compare him to Quinn. I wonder if all oldest children spend their lives making sure everything is okay for their younger siblings. I've never experienced any of that since I am an only child. All of a sudden, I envy Lizabett.

"I got some pistachios," Uncle Lou says as he points to a bowl of nuts he's placed on the counter by the chairs. "Your dad always liked pistachios."

"You spoil us." I smile at Uncle Lou.

Uncle Lou swipes at the counter with a cloth. "He'll be here any minute now. The program starts in a few minutes, and he always likes to get the introduction on programs like that."

It occurs to me that Uncle Lou knows my father even better than I do.

"Did my dad know about my cancer when he left us?" My mouth opens, and the question is out before I even realize I'm going to ask it.

Uncle Lou stops swiping at the counter and darts a glance at me. "Your dad never left you—he left your mother, but not you."

"I just wondered if he knew," I say. Once I asked the question, I realized how very much I wanted to know the answer. It was as though all of the restraint for the past six years was pushing me to finally get the answer.

Uncle Lou moves the bowl of nuts closer to the edge of the counter. "Your dad loves you."

I close my eyes. "Wouldn't he have stayed with us for just a little longer if he knew I had cancer?"

I don't need to open my eyes to know someone has entered the room. Uncle Lou scrapes a chair on the floor as he moves it into place. "We're all set up for the program."

I open my eyes and see my dad walking toward one of the chairs Uncle Lou has set out. My dad had to have heard my question, but he doesn't say anything. I can see him stuff the baseball cap he brought back into his pocket, though. Usually, the first thing he does is put the new cap on my head.

"Maybe you'd like a sandwich while you watch the program today," my uncle says to my dad in this upbeat voice. "Marilee makes a great tuna sandwich. It only takes a minute."

"That'd be nice," my dad says. "I didn't get a chance to have lunch."

My dad hasn't looked either me or Uncle Lou in the eye, and he seems tired.

"I'll be right back with it," I say. I guess I'm not going to get an answer to any of my questions. Besides, I could use a minute or two in the kitchen before I have to face my dad again. Not that I'm crying or anything. My eyes are just a little watery from the eye makeup that I have on.

The program has been on for a good

fifteen minutes, and my dad has finished his sandwich by the time Quinn comes back. I haven't been able to find the enthusiasm to cheer for the old teams that are shown on the "best of baseball greats" so I am glad Quinn is here.

Quinn sits down in a chair next to me.

"Quinn, this is my father. Dad, this is Quinn," I say.

My dad frowns at Quinn as though he needs to decide if he's okay or not.

"Pleased to meet you, sir," Quinn says as he holds out his hand to my father.

My father grunts, but he shakes Quinn's hand. "You a friend of Marilee's?"

"I'm working on it," Quinn says.

"We're just getting to know each other, Dad," I say.

"What does that mean?" Dad says as he squints at us.

My father hasn't been a father to me for the past six years, so I can't think of one good reason why he's decided to act like one now.

"We're doing a few things together, that's all," I say. I can't help it if my voice is a little formal. I don't like it that my father is interfering. He probably hasn't noticed that I'm twenty-five years old now.

"My intentions are honorable, if that's what you want to know," Quinn says with a quick smile.

My dad ignores Quinn and looks at me. "What sort of things are the two of you doing?"

My only excuse for saying what I do next is that I was at the end of my patience. "We're going to church on Sunday."

"Oh."

Well, at least that makes my father stop asking me questions. Knowing how he feels about churches, I'm surprised he doesn't stand up and leave. Instead, he turns to look at Quinn more closely.

"You one of those Christians?" my dad finally asks Quinn.

Quinn nods. "Sure am."

I have to give Quinn points for bravery under fire. My dad scowls at him for a few minutes, but Quinn doesn't let his enthusiastic expression fade.

"It was the Christians who killed all those people in the Crusades," my dad says.

"And it was Christians who put up leprosy

colonies and built orphanages and visited prisons," Quinn replies.

"I hope you don't think Marilee will be doing any of those things. She's had cancer, you know."

"I know," Quinn says.

"She's not as strong as she used to be," my dad adds.

"I'm just fine," I say. "And, if you're worried about me going to church, you can just—"

"—come with us," Quinn interrupts. "There's always room for one more."

"Me?" my dad says, as if Quinn has suggested Dad go swimming with sharks.

Quinn shrugs. "It would be one way for you to know what is going on in church."

My dad frowns. "Well, I've never—I mean—church isn't—"

"I could pick you up here," Quinn says. "Sunday at ten-thirty."

"My dad wouldn't—" I say to Quinn. "I mean, he's not the type to—"

"I'll go," my dad speaks up.

"You will?" I pause. "Go to church?" I pause again. "Mom goes to church."

"Not this one surely?" my dad asks.

"Well, no, not this one," I say. My mom goes to a small church in Arcadia. Quinn has said the church he goes to is in Pasadena.

"Well, then, somebody needs to go with you, so it may as well be me," my dad says as he pulls the baseball cap out of his pocket and hands it to me.

"Oh. Thanks." I don't know what else to say. I like that he finally gave me the cap, but being a father is about more than handing out headgear. If he couldn't be bothered to worry about my cancer, I'm not sure he has the right to worry about things like me and church. Still, I kind of like the thought of us going to church together.

"I won't wear a hat, though," my dad says as he turns to Quinn. "A cap is good enough for me. I'm no executive or anything."

"Not too many men wear hats to church anymore," Quinn says.

My dad grunts. "They did the last time I went. Down South. I always thought it was a foolish thing. You just wear it to the door and then you have to chase it around on the pew for the rest of the time." He pauses. "I could wear a suit, though. I wear one of those to work most days, so that's no problem."

"I could wear a dress," I say.

"Anything is fine," Quinn says. "Suits. Dresses. Slacks. It's pretty casual."

We're halfway through the television program before I realize I have a problem. My Sunday date just evaporated. I'm still going to church with Quinn, but I'm pretty sure the Sisterhood won't count it as a date if my father comes along with us.

I'm beginning to wonder for the umpteenth time if meeting these goals is worth it. I've lost some of my zest for getting a date with the grill guy, and I doubt I'll get another date from Quinn, not after he takes me and my dad to church together. I can't imagine I'll be any fun to be with when my dad is sitting by my side. Quinn will likely be a one-function date.

I look over at Quinn. He doesn't look as if he's had a bad day so far. "Did you talk to Lizabett after you dropped me off earlier?"

Quinn shakes his head. "She's coming down with something, so she didn't feel like talking."

"I thought she might want to talk about how disappointed she is that her ballet performance was canceled," I say.

Quinn frowns. "The theater should never

have let them book that production. They have a dozen violations to fix before they can have a performance of any kind there."

I should stop myself right now, but I don't. "Are you the one who found the violations?"

"No, that was the captain," Quinn says. "I only wish he'd gone over there a week ago, so the girls wouldn't be so disappointed—if they'd had a little advance notice, they could have found another place to have their ballet."

"You should tell that to Lizabett," I say. "That it was the captain."

"What kind of a place do they need?" my dad asks.

I wasn't aware that my dad was following the discussion between Quinn and myself, but I can tell now that both my dad and my uncle have been listening.

"Really all they need is a large space with slick floors for dancing," Quinn says. "I think they only sold fifty or so tickets, so it wouldn't need to be a theater. If they had a space to dance, they could put up folding chairs around it."

"Well, there should be a place like that," I say. I look around the diner. "If our rooms here weren't so chopped up, we'd have room to host something like that."

"Is this for one of your Sisterhood friends?" my dad asks.

I nod. I never thought my dad knew about the Sisterhood. Of course, he's seen Becca sometimes when he's here watching a game—and maybe he's seen Carly and Lizabett once or twice, but I've never mentioned the Sisterhood to him. I look over at Uncle Lou. He must be the one telling my dad things about me.

"When is the ballet happening?" my dad asks.

Uncle Lou must be coaching my dad. He hasn't been involved in my life since he left Mom. To listen to him now, though, you'd think he was the guy on that old television show, *Father Knows Best.* I'm beginning to wonder if he thinks that he can make up for his lack of interest in me for the past six years with a sudden intense involvement in everything surrounding me from my church date with Quinn to the Sisterhood problems.

"We could have a performance at where I work—in our main showroom," my dad says. "We'd have to drive the show cars outside to the back lot, but we do that all the time anyway."

"You could give Lizabett's group a place to do their ballet?" I ask.

My dad nods. "I'm pretty sure. I'd have to clear it with the general manager, but he's a good guy. If I tell him it's for my daughter and her friends, he'll understand."

Understand what? I wonder. I'm surprised anyone at Dad's work even knows he has a daughter.

"What day would you need the place?" my dad asks.

"They had planned on doing their production this coming Wednesday," I say.

My dad nods. "I'll ask. I'm sure it'll be fine."

"My brothers and I would be happy to help—we could set up chairs or move cars or anything," Quinn says. "Lizabett has been looking forward to dancing in this production, and I hate to see her disappointed."

"I'd appreciate it, too," I say.

I'm not used to having my father do anything for me and I'm not sure what to make of it all. I look over and see Uncle Lou beaming at us both as if he'd just taught us to fly, so I figure he's behind this sudden interest my dad has in my life. I wish I felt like beaming. I'm going to need some time to think about all of this, though, before I know what to make of it all.

Chapter Eight

Call me Diana, not Princess Diana.
—Princess Diana

The week after we had our crowns, Lizabett brought in another princess quote.

We giggled about what we would do if we were really princesses.

Lizabett wanted to knight her brothers and send them off to rescue other damsels in distress—with the added request that they bring her back a stuffed dragon or two. Carly said she'd build an all-pink castle by the beach in Malibu—something with turrets so she could look out to the ocean. Becca said she'd have real hot chocolate, none of the mix kind, brought to her every morning on a silver tray along with the New York Times. *Becca likes to know any bad news right away in the morning.*

Castles and chocolate were too rich for me, and I had no desire for any kind of news early in the morning, so I said I'd settle for having a butler. The others teased me about why I would want a butler, but I didn't tell them. In the books I had read, a butler always seemed to stop any unpleasantness at the door. He didn't let trouble into his mistress's house. I figured a good butler could do that in my life. When I thought about it some more, I realized a butler was the closest thing to a father a grown woman can have and still be totally independent.

It wasn't until after my father and Quinn left that Becca came through the doors to The Pews. I must admit things had been so hectic I hadn't given a second thought to the fact that she hadn't answered my call this morning telling her that Carly's cat was still lost. As it turns out, Becca has problems of her own.

Listen to them.

"I can't believe it," Becca says. She sits down at the counter in The Pews and I place a tall glass of iced tea in front of her. It's about nine-thirty at night, and there's no one sitting close to us. Becca is speaking in a low voice anyway. "There just isn't anyone more suited to that internship than me. I swear there isn't. They practically admitted as much when I called."

Becca takes a minute to just stare at the glass of iced tea.

"You called them?" I ask just to keep Becca talking. "The judge herself?"

"No, I couldn't reach the judge," Becca admits as she looks at me instead of the tea. She looks miserable as she puts her hand around the glass. "The only one who would talk to me was the law clerk who runs the internship application process. And he as much as admitted that I was the best candidate. He said there had been only one thing standing between me and getting the internship."

"Well, if it's only one thing, maybe you can change it and—"

"I'm not getting the internship," Becca says. Her knuckles tighten on the glass she's holding. "They're discriminating against me."

"Discriminating?"

Becca nods and lifts the glass of iced tea to her lips. She takes a drink before continuing. "Of course, they won't admit it."

"They can't discriminate against you," I say. By now I am indignant. "That's not fair. Besides, a judge should be open to all religions."

Becca grunts as she sets her glass down on the counter. "They're not discriminating against me because I'm Jewish. It's because of the cancer."

"Oh." This is even more shocking to me. "Can they do that?"

"Of course they can. They can't come out and tell me that's the reason I wasn't chosen, but what else could it be? I have a 4.0 in my classes. The law clerk admitted none of the other candidates have a 4.0 average. Plus, I'm on the debate team. I'm perfect for the internship, and they're not going to give it to me."

Becca's jaw is set.

"Maybe you misunderstood the law clerk," I say. "Maybe he just can't tell you who's gotten the internship yet, and so he's stalling."

"They gave the internships to a Marcia Richards and a Paul Stone. There's only the two. The congratulation letters have already gone out. The consolation letters go out tomorrow. I'll be getting one of those."

"But how would they even know **you** had cancer?"

Becca taps her fingers against the counter. "That friend of my grandfather who knows the judge called and talked to her. He told her about the cancer—said he'd recommend me for anything because he admired me for the way I faced adversity. The law clerk told me that. I suppose he thought it'd make me feel better."

"But, that's good, isn't it? You faced adversity. I would think the judge would want that in an intern."

"The judge wants interns who will live long enough to use what they learn in her court in career situations, and that's after they live long enough to go through law school."

"You're going to live through law school—and longer. You could outlive those other two guys by years and years."

Becca gives me a tight smile. "We don't know that, though, do we?"

"Of course we don't know," I say. Will cancer always haunt us? "But no one really knows how long they have to live. Those other two don't know how long they will live, either."

"It's the odds," Becca says. "The judge was just going with the odds."

"You listen to me, Rebecca Snyder," I say. "You're a fighter. You've beaten the odds. You know what you need to do to stay healthy. You're already ten steps ahead of most people our age."

Becca shrugs. "Tell it to the judge."

"Maybe I will," I say. "Somebody needs to ask the judge or her law clerk or whoever is in the know about this. They can't just go disqualifying people because they don't like their health histories. It can't be right. I'm going to call them."

"They've already gone home for the weekend," Becca says.

"They'll be back at their desks on Monday, and if you're not going to call them, I am."

"I'll call," Becca says. "Besides, they probably wouldn't talk to you anyway. You'd have to be one of the applicants to get them to talk about the internship at all."

"Well," I say as I put my arm around Becca's shoulders, "I don't want you to worry. Once you talk to them, they'll have to add a third internship for the summer."

Becca leans into my hug, and I pat her back. Then she hiccups. She always does that when she's trying not to cry.

"I wish we had the Sisterhood meeting tonight," Becca says.

"We could call an emergency meeting," I say. There have been several times during the years when we've called emergency meetings. Usually when we do that, we don't get any knitting done. We just focus on whatever the problem is.

Becca shakes her head. "I'll be okay. I just need to call them again on Monday. That law clerk knows why I didn't get selected. And if I press him hard enough, he'll tell me the truth."

"You'll let me know when you've talked to him?"

Becca nods. "You can count on it."

Once Becca has talked about her frustrations, she feels better. We talk a little before she decides to do a little shopping and come back to the diner later. She had told Lizabett earlier that she would go to the baseball game with everyone else tomorrow, so she wanted to get some new tennis shoes.

"I'm going to play if they need someone to even out the teams," Becca says.

I had almost forgotten about the ball game when Quinn mentioned it before he left. He is planning to stop by here and pick me and my dad up around eleven in the morning. That's right. My dad has decided to join us at baseball, too, which pretty well disqualifies the baseball game as a date, as well.

Oh, well, I'll have to get some real dates, I guess. In the meantime, I need to get my baseball caps ready for the firemen to use on the table they are setting up. I have most of my caps in my office here, but I'll want to bring in the ones from my room at home, too.

It's almost 10:00 p.m. and we close the diner at eleven on Friday nights. Most of our business is from the lunch and early dinner crowd, so we decided long ago that eleven was late enough for us to keep things open even on the weekends. On weeknights, we close at ten.

"Lizabett said the grill guy is going to the game tomorrow, too," Becca says as she grins at me. She's finished her shopping. "Didn't I tell you he was friendly? He fits right in with the rest of us."

"He probably just wants to do something for the kids, too," I say.

I am careful to keep my voice neutral. I know Becca wants Randy, the grill guy, to ask me out, but I don't think that will happen. If he asks anyone out, it will probably be Carly.

It's too bad Carly and I can't switch goals. I could go to the pound and find a cat that would suit me, and Carly could get all the dates she needed from the grill guy himself. Carly and Randy didn't stop by the diner after I came back, but I got an e-mail message from Carly saying that her cat was still up in the trees around the house. Carly was so worried about her cat getting hungry that she left opened cans of tuna at the bases of several trees before she went inside for the night. She made sure the trees were in her front lawn, however, so that there could be no question about littering.

I go into the kitchen to tell Uncle Lou I am leaving.

"Get Carlos to walk you to the parking garage," Uncle Lou says from the counter. He is chopping up onions for a soup he is making for tomorrow. Carlos washes dishes at The Pews and is always there until closing.

"Becca's walking to the garage, too, so we'll be fine," I say.

If it's after nine at night Uncle Lou has insisted someone walk me to the parking garage ever since I started working for the diner. He does the same for the waitresses.

"But thanks for worrying," I say as I walk over to Uncle Lou and give him a quick hug.

"What's that for?" Uncle Lou says as he looks up from his onion.

"Just because," I say as I leave the kitchen.

Becca has a bit of a drive to get home to the Fairfax district, and I live several miles from The Pews, so we don't stop any place on our walk to the parking garage. The night is dark, but every window along Colorado Boulevard is lit up. We turn right at The Cheesecake Factory and cross the street to go into the parking structure. I'm on the third floor and Becca is on the roof so we agree to both take the elevator to the roof, and she'll drive me down to my car.

I have to admit I am tired tonight. I still haven't figured out my dad, but I do know one thing for sure. I'm not going to tell my mother that dad and I are planning to go to church together on Sunday. She'd have people praying over us all night if she thought anything like that was happening.

I thank Becca when she drops me off at my car. She waits for me to get inside my car and start my engine before she continues to the exit.

My drive home is quiet. I always like driving at night. I do some of my best thinking in the black of night—maybe because there are so few distractions.

So why is my dad taking this sudden interest in me? Oh, I'm pretty sure Uncle Lou has talked to him. Uncle Lou must have talked to him before, so why has it made a difference now? My dad managed to skate through all my cancer years without getting involved in my life, so it's a little late, don't you think?

I'm still fretting about my dad when I pull

my car into the driveway. My mother rents half of a duplex on Walnut Avenue in eastern Pasadena. It's the same house we lived in when my dad lived with us. I wonder all of a sudden why my mother has stayed here. We could have moved years ago when she got that promotion at the bank. She could even buy a place if she wanted. It must be strange for her in this place with memories of Dad all around.

I barely finish asking the question before I remember the times when my mother has asked me how I feel about where we live. I always told her I was comfortable here. I wonder if that's why she's never moved.

Of course, I realize, that is why we've never moved. I wonder how many other sacrifices Mom has made for me without making a big deal about them.

And look at me. I can't even look Mom in the eye tonight when she asks me to go to church with her on Sunday. She always asks me so faithfully, and she's actually pretty nice about it. She doesn't make me feel guilty for not going with her or anything. She might tell me the topic of the sermon or some special hymn that's planned, but she doesn't nag. Really, I should have gone with her a long time ago. It's a small thing to do after she's done so much for me.

If I weren't already going to church with Quinn and Dad, I'd go with Mom this Sunday. Speaking of which…

"What's the name of your church again?" I ask, just to be sure there is no confusion on my part. I cannot even begin to imagine Mom's reaction if my dad and I walked into her church by mistake on Sunday. On second thought, I can imagine. But she confirms that it's not Quinn's church.

I look at my mom and I see a face that has been around me all my life. It's not a beautiful face, but it's a nice face. Brown hair with some gray in it. Green eyes behind glasses. It's a face that softens when she looks at me.

My mom would be hurt if she saw Dad and me come into church with someone else—and, with us not even having had the courtesy to tell her that we were coming. I promise myself I will tell Mom about the two of us going to church just as soon as we have done it. I don't want to get her hopes up in case something happens and we don't go.

I give Mom a hug just like the one I gave Uncle Lou earlier. She wonders what it is for just like he did.

I shrug. "No special reason."

Well, what can I say? That I'm finally growing up?

I go to bed feeling pretty good considering I'm bringing down the average for the Sisterhood in terms of meeting goals. Going to church with Quinn and my dad might not count as a date, but it's a big step for me and I'm glad I'm finally taking it. I wonder if God will remember me and all those things I said about Him when I had my cancer. If He does, I hope He has a sense of humor. It would help if He knew a little about knitting, too.

I get to The Pews early Saturday morning so I can go to my office and pack all of my baseball caps in the small duffel bag I have. I'm not wearing any of the caps because I have used some mousse on my hair this morning, and I don't want my hair to get flattened under a cap. These caps might be the stuff that champions are made of, but they don't send out the kind of message I need to send if I'm going to get more dates before next Thursday.

I probably won't be able to write in the journal while the baseball game is going on, but I'll do what I can to let you know what is happening. And I can certainly check my e-mail to see if Carly has an update on her cat.

Oh, yes, here's an e-mail from Carly: Tuna gone. All four cans. At least Marie isn't hungry. She's still up in the tree, though. I saw her this morning. She moved to one of the trees inside the fence. I guess that's because that's where I put the tuna. Randy says we should go to the baseball game with all of you—he says Marie is playing hard to get, and she'll come down quicker if we ignore her a little. Anyway, Randy and I will both be at the game. See you then. Oh—I just reread this and I know what you're thinking, but you'd be wrong. Randy did go home last night. He just came back early this morning. Marilee, you really need to date this guy. He's nice.

Now that I've added Carly's e-mail for

you, I have to tell you my reponse is "No comment." Randy might be nice, but he's clearly interested in Carly and her cat. Don't you think? Not that it matters, I hear Quinn talking to Uncle Lou out front so I'd better put my pen away and go out there.

Okay, I'm back—now we're up at the park in Altadena. It's a great park next to the foothills, and there are lots of kids here. White kids. Blacks. Hispanics. Armenians. Asians. The whole melting pot, and they're all ready to play ball. The reason I have a few minutes to write in the journal is because our team is up to bat and I won't be going up for some time. I wouldn't bother to write at a time like this normally, but I have to tell someone how I am feeling, and you're it. I particularly don't want to let Lizabett see that I am upset.

Lizabett is on my team, by the way, and she's getting ready to go up to bat after two more players go. You should see Lizabett this morning—she's bouncy and happy because Quinn told her that my dad was going to see if the car dealership where he works will let her ballet company use their showroom for the production of *Swan Lake.*

I've had to watch my face because Lizabett keeps smiling over at me as if we have a wonderful secret. I'm afraid the secrets go deeper than she knows. I feel as though I have one of my own and I can't tell her. You see, my dad didn't show up this morning for the baseball game. He didn't call me or Quinn or Uncle Lou and tell us he wasn't coming to The Pews to meet us to ride to the game; he just didn't show. We waited around for twenty minutes for him, but then we had to leave. Quinn told Uncle Lou where the park was so my father could drive up when he got to the diner.

Oh, we handled it well. Uncle Lou said my dad had probably gotten caught in some weekend traffic. I said he might have had car trouble. We all smiled and agreed something unforeseen must have come up.

Inside I knew better. I'm in on the secret. My dad didn't come because he's doing what he always does—he's flaking out. He's busy making commitments he won't keep and promises he'll ignore. It's as if he thinks that if a commitment isn't important to him, it's not important to anyone else, either.

That's why I'm finding it so hard to return Lizabett's smiles. She's all happy because she thinks my father has solved her problem; I'm the only one who knows her problems are just what they always were. My dad won't do what he said he would do. Lizabett is no closer to having a place for her ballet performance than she was yesterday when she first heard the old theater was closed. In fact, she might be further away than she was yesterday, because she's wasting time today thinking she has a solution when she could be out there looking for another place.

You see why I'm so upset? I don't want Lizabett to be disappointed, and I particularly don't want it to be my father who disappoints her. I'm used to the way my father operates, but Lizabett is not. She expects my dad to be like Quinn and, let's face it, Quinn would move mountains with his bare hands to make Lizabett happy. My dad is not like that. He's not even close.

Well, you get the idea. I'm glad I can write my thoughts down in this journal.

Oh, there's Lizabett now, and she's up to bat. She doesn't look much bigger than some of the kids here, but she does know how to swing a bat. See there, she's got it and she's off to first base.

Quinn is walking over here now, so I'm going to close for a bit. He's the assistant to the assistant coach for the other team, and he's coming over to get some more bottles of water. It would bother some guys to be the assistant to the assistant, but Quinn looks perfectly happy to just be the guy who gets everyone their water. He's looking at me now, and I can see he's going to stop and say hi before he picks up the water bottles that he needs.

You know, with the sun shining behind Quinn's head as it is right now, I'd say he's even better-looking than the grill guy. Don't tell the others that I said that or they'll be after me to get some more dates out of him before next Thursday, and I have to tell you I'm losing my drive to date Quinn like that—not that I don't want to go out with him, but I don't want to do it just to finish up some goals. A guy like Quinn deserves better than that. Of course, I'm making major assumptions here. He might not want to really date me at all, especially not when my father completely lets Lizabett down.

Yeah, that could be a problem all right. I wonder if Uncle Lou knows anyone who has enough room for a production of *Swan Lake*. He knows all the restaurant people along the boulevard—maybe one of them will have room enough. I can hope, at least, can't I?

Oh, here's Quinn. Gotta go.

Chapter Nine

Acting should be bigger than life.
Scripts should be bigger than life.
It should all be bigger than life.
—Bette Davis

We had one Sisterhood meeting that first year when we didn't knit. It was the meeting after Lizabett had surgery on her leg. We had all braced ourselves for the surgery, knowing Lizabett was so frail she could die from the surgery alone. We were pulling for her so hard that we didn't know what to do when the doctors said they'd have to do a second surgery.

Lizabett had already taken chemotherapy

to reduce the size of her tumor before the first operation, so she was in bad shape. I didn't think she looked strong enough to live through another surgery. All of the Sisterhood felt that way, except for Lizabett. The Old Mother Hen had told her she'd be fine, and she believed him. She wasn't afraid.

That's why Becca brought the rest of us this acting quote. Lizabett was in the hospital that week, and so wasn't with us at our meeting. We knew we needed to hide our worries from her when we went to visit her just like The Old Mother Hen hid his. I soon discovered that some of the best acting never makes it onto the movie screen. Instead, it's played out next to hospital beds all across the country.

My baseball caps are popular with the kids. The Los Angeles Dodgers. The Toronto Blue Jays. The Cincinnati Reds. I have all their caps and more sitting on a folding table with the brims all facing upward. The table looks like it has dozens of colorful bumps on it.

The kids all crowded around the table earlier until it was time for them to put on their T-shirts—one team was blue and one was red. Then they hit the field. I was on a team, but, when my team was up to bat, I sat on a bench by the table holding my caps and watching the game.

The game was almost over when the little girl came up to me and asked me where I got all the caps. I noticed this girl earlier, although she hadn't gathered around the table like the other kids had then. Instead, she'd spent the time before the game walking beside Quinn and talking to him as he pulled the cart of water bottles back and forth to where the teams would be sitting. The little girl was Hispanic and looked as though she was seven or eight years old.

"What's your name?" I ask the girl as I put my hand on her shoulder.

She leans into me as if she was starved for affection. "Lupe."

"Well, Lupe," I say as I bend down to put my arm around her shoulders, "my dad gave me these caps."

Her eyes grow serious. "My dad doesn't give me any caps. He's in prison."

I squeeze her shoulder. "That's too bad."

"I wish he wasn't in prison," she says. "My mom misses him."

"I'm sure she does." I wonder if my mom ever misses my dad. I suppose she does sometimes.

"I miss him, too," Lupe says.

I nod. I don't tell her that sometimes a dad doesn't need to be in prison for his daughter to miss him.

Instead, I give Lupe my Baltimore Orioles cap. I noticed her looking at that one in particular, and she admitted she liked the bird on the cap. She said she likes birds because they can fly away when they want and no one can ever keep them in a prison—I decided not to tell her about cages.

After I give Lupe her cap, she runs to show it to Quinn.

That just happened a minute ago, so I now have a few minutes to write in this journal. Usually I just note things here and there, but my conversation with Lupe has struck a few chords with me. If I'm not careful, I'll write a whole editorial right here and now about how much daughters need to have their fathers around.

If you could have seen the longing on Lupe's face, I wouldn't even need to write a word for you to agree with me. She likes the cap I gave to her, but, even that does not make her eyes sparkle with complete joy. Talking about her dad has made her lonely.

Thinking about my dad has made me feel lonely, too. Especially because I can look out over the baseball field here and see Lizabett with her smiling confidence in my father and Quinn, who really believes my father had car trouble this morning. It's as if they know a man who doesn't exist.

The way I have coped with my father during all the years since I got cancer is that I expect nothing from him. Zero. Nada. If I expect nothing, I am never disappointed. And, then, if he does come by the diner to see me, I can be pleased because it is something instead of nothing.

If he gives me a half hug instead of a full hug, I can be happy.

I'm not sure I can continue like this, though.

Something about writing this journal is making me less content with the way I used to handle things. Maybe when I see it all written out in black and white, I see how very small our contact has been all along. Even prisoners are allowed some visits with their families. My dad could be in prison like Lupe's and spend more time with me than he does.

There's not much more to say to that, so I look up just in time to see Lizabett hit the ball. Wham—right over to the right field. And she's off and running to first base. I can hear Quinn cheering louder than anyone else. The game should be over in a few minutes, and then Quinn is planning to take me out for coffee.

I have already decided that I am not going to count coffee with Quinn or the walk in the dark to look for Carly's cat last night as dates toward my goal. It feels a little pressured and contrived to go out on dates just to meet a goal, and I want this thing with Quinn to be its own thing. If I'm going to date a guy just to meet a goal, I'd rather it be some stranger who isn't my friend.

Becca isn't going to understand this, of course. Maybe if I can find a place for Lizabett's ballet troupe to give their performance,

Becca will forgive me. At least we will meet *that* goal. And there's nothing that says I can't get three dates yet. After all, I haven't really turned on my charm. Who knows what might happen?

Speaking of romance, here comes Carly now. She and Randy just got to the park, and Carly's walking toward me looking as if she's lost her last friend. I see Randy walk over to the bench where Quinn's team is sitting.

Watching Carly walk toward me reminds me that I should tell you again what a beautiful day it is here. It is February and so the air is clear—we have enough Santa Ana winds to blow the smog away. The grass here in the park is that deep mature green that says the park is well-tended year-around. I think the grass was mowed this morning, as it still has that cut-grass smell.

"How's it going?" I ask Carly.

She plops herself down on the bench next to me. "Sorry we missed most of the game."

"No problem. The blue team is ahead four to three."

I notice Carly hasn't answered my question

about how things are going. "Did your cat come down from the trees?"

"Almost," Carly says. "Randy thinks we need to get one of those little boxes and put a can of tuna in it tonight—you know the boxes where a door slams down while the cat is inside and eating?"

"That might work."

"I couldn't do that to my cat." Carly turns to me with horror on her face. "No one should be boxed in."

"But it would be for Marie's own good. So that she can go back inside where she'll be warm and safe."

"I don't think Marie wants to go inside." Carly says. She sounds forlorn. "Some things just aren't meant to be."

"Well, your cat can't stay outside forever. What does Randy think?"

I see tears start to form in Carly's eyes. She blinks them back quickly. "What does Randy know?"

I don't like the look on Carly's face. She is clearly upset about something. "Did Randy say something to you that upset you?"

Carly smiles. Well, it's not a real smile,

but it shows all her teeth, and I know she means it to be a smile.

"Because if Randy did say something," I continue, "we don't have to hang around with him, you know—none of us do."

It had never occurred to me in all of the years since I met Randy that he might be a mean person. Wouldn't that be something if I spent all that time back then whining about a missed date with an unpleasant guy?

"He's not mean," Carly says. "He's actually a very nice guy."

"Well, that's good," I say.

My attention is taken away from Carly when I hear another cheer. Someone on the blue team hit the ball way out into right field. I stand up to shout and clap like everyone else is doing before I see that the player who hit the ball like that is Becca. "Go, Becca, go!"

As I stand up, the journal falls to the ground in front of our bench. Carly bends over to pick it up. "Mind if I write a little?"

"Be my guest," I say, and decide Carly might like some time alone while she writes. "I'll go give Becca a hug."

* * *

Hi, this is Carly. I have to talk to someone, and I can't tell anyone in the Sisterhood about this so I'm going to tell you. Once I write this down, I'm going to double-fold the pages back and clip them together somehow. Warning—if anyone in the Sisterhood has managed to read this far, you need to stop right now! No peeking.

And the rest of you who are reading this have to promise not to tell anyone else what I'm going to tell you now.

I don't know what to do. We don't have any rules in the Sisterhood about dating, but we should. No Sister should be allowed to date another Sister's boyfriend—or even potential boyfriend. It's just not right. Besides, I wouldn't hurt one of the Sisters for all of the dates in the world, and two women going after the same man is bound to hurt somebody big-time.

My problem is that Randy—Marilee's grill guy—asked me out. And not on a date like getting together for a cup of coffee or even a movie. Those kinds of dates might not really be dates at all. What Randy invited me to do was to have dinner with him at The Dining Room in The Ritz-Carlton Hotel here in Pasadena. That's one of the most expensive restaurants in all of Pasadena. There's no mistaking that for anything but a date.

That place is my aunt's kind of place—elegant and dripping in crystal. It has entrées like sautéed monkfish and poached lobster with desserts like toasted meringue and lavender cream. I know because my aunt has bragged about eating there. It is a hundred dollars to eat there—per person. *Gourmet* magazine voted it one of the World's Best Hotel Dining Rooms.

My aunt would die if I went there on a date.

Of course, she can never even know it was an option. I'm not going to tell anyone about that invitation. I wish Randy had never asked me. I was having a good time with him, waiting for my cat to come down out of the tree. And then he had to spoil it all by asking me out.

You know I can't date Randy. He's Marilee's grill guy. She saw him first. She might even love him now that she's had a chance to get to know him again. I've noticed she has a dreamy look about her sometimes when she's writing in this journal and, when I see her like that, I wonder if she's writing about how nice the grill guy is even after all of these years.

Marilee deserves the grill guy. She's smart. And funny. And brave. I'm not going to stand in the way of her happiness. Who am I kidding? A guy like Randy isn't for me anyway. I'll tell you why sometime, but for now I'll just say there are big reasons. So I told Randy he had to ask Marilee out and not me.

Ah, well. I hope my cat climbs down out of those trees soon. I have a feeling I'm going to need something to hug before this is all over. Randy hasn't talked to me since I suggested he ask Marilee out.

Sometimes life just doesn't work out the way anyone thinks it should.

I'm going to say goodbye now and fold these pages over so many times there will be no chance they'll ever be opened by mistake. I wonder if I can find a stapler somewhere.

I look out to the park, but all I see are dozens of kids milling around in their blue and red T-shirts. The ball game must be over. I wonder what the score is. I see Randy over there carrying water bottles with Quinn.

Randy doesn't look brokenhearted the way you would think a guy would look if a woman he was really interested in said she wouldn't go out with him. Not that I want him to break down in despair or anything, but it does seem a little cold to look quite so cheerful, don't you think? I'm not sure how I feel about that.

This is Marilee again. I'm glad to see Carly wrote her heart out again even if it is highly secretive—I had to cross my heart and promise not to look at any of the pages no matter what. I don't know what the secrecy is for—I know she's still worried about her cat. I hope we find that beast before too much more time goes by. As I've said earlier, Carly tends to be a worrier, and I don't like to see all this tension on her face.

At least she went over to give Becca a congratulatory hug so she's not still sitting on the bench here bemoaning the fact that her cat won't come home.

I, of course, plan to sit here and bemoan entirely different things. My problem is I don't know what to do with myself now. Quinn had said he wanted to take me out for a cup of coffee after the game, but I'm not sure if he means to invite everyone else, too, so I don't want to go running over to Quinn looking as though I'm expecting something special. Because I'm not.

The number of people at the table can make a big difference in whether this is a date or not and I want to be cool about it all until I see if Quinn is collecting other people for coffee, as well. Right now, he's talking to Becca, so you never know.

You may know what to do in this situation and think I'm being silly, but I have been out of the dating game for years and I am just beginning to realize how complicated this whole dating thing is. There is something to be said for arranged marriages, although, believe me, I'm not saying we should go there. It's just that dating is so hazy it's sometimes hard to know if one is out on a date or if one is just passing the time with a guy who thinks you're a buddy.

The only clue as to whether something is a date or not, that I have noticed, is that both people turn their cell phones off when they are on a real date. If they are just friends going out, each of them will take calls from everyone else.

I see Quinn walking toward me now. Of course, I can't see whether or not his cell phone is on. And, unless someone calls him, I will never know whether it is on or off.

Anyway, I have to go. I'll write more after the coffee. Wish me luck.

Oh. Lizabett has joined Quinn as he's walking toward me. I love Lizabett like a sister—well, she is my sister in a way. But I hope I can have some time alone with Quinn just to see if this having coffee together even feels like a date. I wouldn't hurt Lizabett's feelings for the world, but I wonder if she'd like to write some in the journal while Quinn and I have coffee. She seems to like doing that. That doesn't sound as if I'm putting her off, does it? I hope not.

Hi, this is Lizabett. It seems that everybody has been folding back their pages in this journal for a while now. Pretty soon you will be the only one able to read it. It's for sure no one in the Sisterhood will be able to read the whole thing. Of course, I can't complain because I'm going to fold my pages back, too.

I'm sitting at a table in this coffee shop in Altadena called the Coffee Gallery. They call it a gallery because they have paintings on the walls that are for sale and they serve Italian sodas as well as tea and coffee. I'm sitting at a table at one end of the coffee place and Quinn and Marilee are sitting at the other end. There are lots of plants around and the tables are old wood ones. I told Quinn and Marilee I wanted some space to think and write in the journal. They bought it, so I'm back here trying to look literary.

You already know I am excited that the two of them seem to be hitting it off. I can hear them laughing now. Quinn needs to laugh more.

I should apologize about what I wrote about Quinn before—about him hovering over me and condemning that theater in Sierra Madre just so I wouldn't perform and worry him. He wasn't the one who closed the place—you might know that by now. Marilee's father is going to ask his general manager if we can put the production on in their car showroom.

My life is actually going pretty well since it looks as if the ballet production will go on. I'm going to try to look a little tormented, though, just in case Marilee glances back here and wonders why I'm not writing anything down in the journal. When everything is good, there's not much to say. Oh, Quinn is laughing again—a belly laugh this time.

I would love to have Marilee as a sister-in-law. I'm going to keep my cool and not presume too much on what will happen, but they do seem to be getting along quite well. I wish you could see them. Ah, there's another laugh.

Chapter Ten

Keep your face to the sunshine and you cannot see the shadow.

—Helen Keller

We knew we were recovering from our cancers when we started to long for the sun and the sand. Becca brought in a boom box and a CD with the sounds of the ocean when she brought in this quote. Too much sunshine might cause cancer, but to us, that night, sunshine meant life. We all talked about our favorite places to go to the beach around here. Becca liked the Santa Monica pier. Carly talked about Dana Point. Lizabett voted for Malibu. I liked them all.

The next week Rose brought us each a large conch shell—the ones that make a sound like the ocean when you put them to your ear. We spent most of the meeting just listening to those sounds and wondering if we'd ever feel the beach sun on our skin in the same way again.

I hadn't thought about those shells for a long time. What made them so special for me was that I had been thinking about death and the shells seemed so alive. You might think that someone with cancer would automatically think about death, but being afraid of death and thinking about it are not the same things.

No part of me wanted to die—I'd seen enough to know dying is a messy business—but I couldn't help but wonder what being dead would be like. I wondered if there really could be a heaven. I didn't want to think about whether there could also be a hell so I didn't even ask myself that question.

But I did wonder about heaven. Would everything be all white—maybe we'd be dropped in a desert with nothing but white sand for as far as we could see and even the sky would be bleached white? Wouldn't there at least be color in heaven? And grass and trees? And rain?

And what would we be when we were in heaven? Would we be bodies or would we be something all vague and wispy, like the ghosts I'd seen waltzing in the ballroom at the Haunted House in Disneyland? Would we be able to eat? Would we find anything to laugh about? I couldn't imagine living forever with no good jokes or trees or clouds in the sky.

I had been tempted to go to church with Mom just to see if anyone talked about heaven. I must admit that, as I got dressed to go to church on Sunday with Quinn, I was hoping someone would talk about heaven even though the urgency of knowing about it had lessened since it appeared I'd live a good, long life before I needed to worry about it all.

I drove to The Pews around ten o'clock so I would have time to do a few things there before Quinn picked me up to go to church.

That's where I am now. You should see

me. I have a black swirly skirt on and one of those tops with the filmy material that bunches along the center seam—you probably need to see this to know what I mean, but, trust me, it looks good, especially in the raspberry sorbet color I have. I squirted mousse on my hair and used my curling iron so my hair looks as cute as it gets. I have makeup and some cool shoes on.

I already figure my dad won't be joining us for church despite what he said, but I'm surprised when Uncle Lou says my father is sick.

"Well, at least he called," I say. I notice a guilty look on Uncle Lou's face. "He did call, didn't he?"

"Well, he was going to call," Uncle Lou says. "I just beat him to it."

I nod. I wonder how Uncle Lou can keep making excuses for him. "I hope he at least has called his general manager to ask about using the main display floor for the ballet performance."

Uncle Lou shrugs. "I can put in a call to my VFW hall." That's the Veterans of Foreign Wars—Uncle Lou fought in Vietnam. "That floor there might be big enough."

"That place reeks of cigarette smoke—these are little girls in pink leotards. I don't think—"

Uncle Lou nods slowly. "I guess you're right."

If grass were smooth, I would suggest they just have an outdoor production at the park where we were yesterday. But I doubt anyone can pirouette on grass. Besides, it might be cold by then. February weather around here ranges from fairly warm to fairly chilly. We're in a warm spell now, but that won't necessarily last.

"We're going to need to tell Lizabett pretty soon if my dad doesn't arrange anything," I say. I'm not looking forward to that conversation.

Uncle Lou sighs. "Your dad wants to help."

I don't even answer that. If he really wanted to, he would. Isn't it that simple?

The door opens and Quinn comes in, so Uncle Lou and I stop talking about my dad.

Wow. I thought Quinn looked good in his fireman's uniform, but he looks even better in his church clothes. He's wearing tan Dockers and a white shirt that's open at the neck. The reason it all looks so good is that you can really tell Quinn has a tan. I know, I know, tans shouldn't be attractive because we shouldn't encourage people to spend that much time in the sun, but tell that to my eyeballs.

"My dad won't be coming with us," I say just so I get it said up front. I don't say he's sick.

"Oh," Quinn says. "I was hoping to talk to him about the performance."

"I'm going to call some more places," I say.

I remember the Pasadena City Hall. If they have finished the remodeling on their building, I think we could hold a performance there after business hours. They have a very small rental fee, and the floors in the courtyard are marble.

I notice out of the corner of my eye that Uncle Lou heads back into the kitchen. We don't have any customers in The Pews, which is unusual, but maybe Uncle Lou needs to stir the soup or something.

"Don't worry. We'll think of a place," I say.

Usually, the sun would be pouring in the windows facing Colorado Boulevard. But I had closed some of the blinds when I first got here, so there's a very mellow light here now—sort of a twilight feeling with enough light to see the shine on the brass rack over the counter and the gleam of the wood all around. The Pews always seems to have atmosphere and it's not letting me down now. "It's too bad this place isn't bigger."

"I'm not worried about finding a place," Quinn says as his eyes crinkle up. I barely have time to register that The Old Mother Hen isn't worried before he continues. "And you look very nice."

Well, I hadn't seen that coming. It's nice to get a compliment.

"I thought I should dress up for church," I say. I'm not going to pretend with Quinn that I've been to church often—only those few times with my mom before dad left—but I don't want him to think I'm a complete heathen who doesn't know that going to church is different than hunting for a runaway cat. "By the way, you look good, too."

I don't know how long we stand there and look at each other until Quinn takes a step closer to me and reaches up to touch my hair. "I like this."

"I decided not to wear a cap." I'm not sure I can breathe right.

Quinn takes his hand and cups my face. "I can see that."

I could say that I didn't see the kiss coming either, but I would be lying. I wanted it to come enough to see it coming even if it wasn't—if that makes any sense. It probably doesn't. I can't think straight enough to make sense.

Quinn's lips are soft, but there is nothing soft about his kiss. I swear my heart is beating so fast Uncle Lou must be able to hear it in the kitchen.

And then, the kiss is over. Quinn still has his arms around me, though, which is nice.

"Is that—I mean should we do that before we go to church?" I say. Maybe heaven won't be the only question I have when I go to church this morning.

Quinn chuckles. "I think God's good with it."

I hear the phone ringing in the kitchen and Uncle Lou answering it. Quinn is still holding me in the circle of his arms and I think I've forgotten how to move.

"Marilee—phone," Uncle Lou calls from the kitchen.

I'm tempted to tell Uncle Lou to have them call me back, but it might be Carly. Or Lizabett. Or Becca. I guess I need to move whether I want to or not. "Sorry."

Quinn steps back a little so I'm not inside his arms any longer. "We need to be going pretty soon anyway."

I nod. I guess we can't stand in The Pews all day and kiss even if there are no customers around.

I manage to walk into the kitchen and even register the fact that Uncle Lou is making his famous chili.

"Hello," I say into the phone.

"Marilee?" a guy's voice asks.

"Yes."

"This is Randy—Randy Parker."

I'm expecting one of the Sisters, so I'm surprised and don't answer right away.

"You know, the guy who's going to do the grill for your uncle?"

"Of course, I know. Hi, Randy."

I stop myself from asking if Carly is okay. I can't think of any other reason for the grill guy to call me.

"Did you find Carly's cat?"

Randy grunts. "That cat doesn't have sense

enough to come down out of that tree no matter what."

Randy doesn't sound too happy with the cat.

"Oh. Well, I hope for Carly's sake it does."

Randy grunts again.

Randy doesn't sound too happy about anything this morning, but I don't know what it has to do with me.

"Say, I was wondering if you'd like to grab a cup of coffee with me tonight," Randy finally says.

"Oh. Sure." He has caught me by surprise.

"There's that coffee place in De Lacey Alley."

"I know the one."

"It's a good place to talk," Randy says. "How does eight o'clock work?"

"Fine. It works fine."

I hang up the phone before I can ask myself if I've just agreed to go on a date with the grill guy. I always thought if I ever had another chance to go out with the grill guy, my life would burst into celebratory fireworks. I'd finally be able to meet my destiny. I'd be ecstatic. Time would swirl around me and I wouldn't notice it.

What I notice now is that my feet hurt. I guess my destiny isn't as much fun as I always thought it would be. My only consolation is that a date is rather hard to define these days.

"It's not really a date," I find myself telling Quinn when I go back out into the main room of The Pews and tell him about the conversation. I wouldn't have even told him about the conversation if I hadn't been so rattled and he wasn't so easy to talk to.

"Not a date?" Quinn grunts. "I wouldn't count on that."

"He probably just wants to talk about Carly's cat," I say. I don't know which one of us—me or Quinn—that I am reassuring.

Quinn grunts even louder at this one. "That guy doesn't care about some cat in a tree."

"But the cat's lost," I say. I notice The Pews isn't as warm and cozy as it was a few minutes ago. Quinn isn't as friendly, either.

"And she's having the time of her life now that she's getting four cans of tuna delivered to her doorstep every night."

Quinn isn't even smiling at me now.

"Well, maybe he wants to talk about the

cat's diet then. I'm not sure a cat should eat that much tuna. It's not tuna in water, either—it's the oil kind. The poor thing will get fat."

I can see Quinn starting to smile. He moves his lips, but his eyes don't warm up and crinkle as they did earlier. "Well, in that case, maybe it is the cat's diet he wants to talk about. We wouldn't want 'the poor thing' falling out of a tree because of her weight."

I nod my head. I suddenly hope I am right and that Randy does want to talk about the cat. "Besides, I'm sure he'll leave his cell phone on. He wouldn't want to miss any calls."

Quinn shrugs. "Eight o'clock, you say? Maybe I should call him around then."

I smile at that. "That'd be okay if you did. You won't be interrupting anything but a talk about tuna."

Now I see Quinn's real smile. "Maybe I'll remind him that it's supposed to be colder tonight and that the cat should be inside. Maybe he'll leave early to go get it down out of that tree once and for all."

We drive to church in Quinn's car. I saw his car the other day when he came to Carly's house and the policeman was writing us tickets for littering. Quinn has a nice sound system in his car and a classical CD plays for us.

I'll admit I am a little nervous about going to church, but I am comfortable with Quinn beside me. He greets a few people in front of the church and then we go inside.

I don't know what to expect, but the church is nice.

It doesn't have any of those fancy stained-glass windows, and I'm a little disappointed about that, but there is a beautiful wooden cross in the front of the church and the windows along the side of the church are made out of a coated glass so that light shines through but no one can see through the window. There are long pews made out of wood and a maroon carpet that covers the entire floor even the area up by the pulpit and where the organ is.

I only have a minute to take it all in before people come over to where Quinn and I are standing. Quinn introduces me to everyone. I won't remember half of their names, but I will remember how friendly everyone is.

The church service starts with a hymn, and I am surprised that I can follow along pretty well because they have a screen up front with all of the words to the song. Quinn has a nice bass voice, and it's kind of fun to sing. The song we sing has the word *Hallelujah* in it a lot and so it has a happy sound to it.

Actually, the whole service is happy. The minister talks about the faith that led Moses to cross the Red Sea and I have to admit I am impressed. I'm not sure I would have the nerve to cross the wet ground where the sea used to be, especially when the sea walls were high above my head, but I've got to admire Moses for doing it. It would be kind of like doing Splash Mountain at Disneyland, only without the cart. Moses was some man.

I'm disappointed because there is no mention of heaven, but all in all, it wasn't bad. I wonder if my mother's church is as happy as this one is and I hope it is. It's been so long since I've been there that I can't remember. I'd like to picture her in a place like this when she goes off on Sunday.

The closing prayer is happening before I

know it and it suddenly occurs to me that I've been almost as brave as Moses today because I've gone to church. I mean, it's not doing Splash Mountain without a cart, but the walls didn't collapse on me and no one pointed a finger at me and asked me what I was daring to do here. No, it was okay.

Quinn is taking me up to meet the minister before I can stop him.

"Oh, you've brought a guest today," the minister says to Quinn and then he turns to me. The minister is a man of about sixty. "We're happy to have you with us, Miss…?"

"Davidson," I say. "Marilee Davidson."

"If there's anything the church can do for you, don't hesitate to let me know." The minister shakes my hand. "My name's Pastor Engstrom, by the way."

Wow. That's a pretty big offer. "Do many people ask for help?"

"Some," the minister says. He keeps talking to me while he shakes Quinn's hand. "And sometimes people just have questions. I never mind trying to answer a question."

I don't know when I will go to a church

next so I figure now is my chance. "Are any of the questions about heaven?"

The minister nods. He's focused completely on me now. "Some people just wonder what it will be like."

"Do you think there will be trees?"

The minister smiles. His eyes don't waver from mine even though a line of handshakers is forming behind Quinn and me. "I think we'll have all of the good things we love down here up there—it's just that things will be bigger and better."

That sounded okay to me.

"I tell people it's going to be like switching from black-and-white to full-color television," the minister adds. "It's not so much that everything will be unfamiliar, it will just be more wonderful than anything we've seen before."

Well, that's even better. I watched enough daytime television when I was sick to know what black-and-white looked like. There were enough old reruns to give me a real good idea of how people must have felt when they saw their first color television program.

"If you have more questions, I have a group of people who come to my office early

Thursday mornings to learn about the Bible. You're welcome to join us."

"I'm not a Christian," I say.

The minister shrugs. "Neither are half of them. They're just curious."

That doesn't sound so bad. "Well, I'm certainly curious."

The minister smiles. "See you Thursday at eight o'clock. My office is to the side of the main part of the church. Can't miss it."

"Okay," I say.

The minister shakes my hand again and, before you know it, Quinn and I are outside in the open air.

I must admit I am pleased with how this whole going-to-church thing went.

"Church was easy," I say to Quinn as we walk to the parking lot.

Quinn looks over at me. "I'm not sure it's meant to be easy."

"Well, if you want people to come and join you, it should be easy."

We are standing beside Quinn's car and he opens the passenger door for me. "Take that Bible course with the pastor for a month or so and you'll know why it isn't so easy."

"I don't think you should be discouraging me."

Quinn grins. "I'm not discouraging you—I'm trying to make it sound intriguing. I'm afraid you might be bored if it sounds easy."

You know, Quinn is right. I'm a little surprised to realize it. Being easy was one of my problems all along with heaven. It just sounded too boring and easy. I much prefer a little Splash Mountain thrown in. I'm kind of glad church isn't really as easy as I thought.

Quinn takes me to a place that has Chinese food and we have egg rolls and shrimp in black bean sauce for lunch.

"What's your fortune cookie say?" Quinn asks.

I read the white paper. "I will find new insights if I look closely."

I look across the table at Quinn, wondering if I will find new insights about him. It's a lazy Sunday afternoon and I'm not sure I want new insights. I'm still pondering the old ones—well, the ones from this morning at any rate.

Insight number one is that Quinn is a good kisser. Insight number two is that I'm not so very happy to be going out with the grill guy tonight.

Isn't that just how life is? When you get the guy you've wanted forever, you want someone new—even if that someone new might not be interested in you now that the guy you wanted forever has asked you out for coffee.

It takes me a moment to notice that Quinn is holding his fortune, too.

"How about yours? What does it say?"

Quinn chuckles. "It says a friend will give me great riches."

"I think that was supposed to be my fortune cookie," I say.

"There's nothing wrong with insights."

I wonder if Quinn would still say that if he knew I was looking at him, hoping for those insights. I am very aware that Quinn is not the usual kind of a guy. I'm not sure I've ever met a man like him.

I suddenly hope the friend who's going to give him great riches isn't some other woman.

Chapter Eleven

If we would build on a sure foundation
in friendship, we must love friends for
their sakes rather than for our own.
—Charlotte Bronte

The odd thing about the Sisterhood is that we never talked much about the bond between us. We talked about everything else—our cancer, our fears, our hopes. But we never talked about our growing friendship, not even on the night when Rose brought this quote to us.

At first, I thought it was because we worried that, if we talked about it, the bond growing between us would dissolve and blow away like dust. Finally, I realized it wasn't that at all. We didn't talk about our friendship because it was the one sure rock in our shifting landscape. We didn't need to talk about it; we didn't need to question it or applaud it. It was just there. We were the Sisterhood. That's all we needed to know.

Don't ask me why I'm thinking about friendship tonight while I'm in my office getting ready to meet the grill guy, but I am—big-time. Maybe it's because I'm looking at this journal. You know, the one you're reading. It's just a notebook kind of a journal with a cardboard aqua cover like something you would use in school.

The thing I'm noticing about the notebook now, though, is how many pages have been folded down or clipped shut so that no one else can read them. Those are all secret pages and we've never had secrets in the Sisterhood before.

I'm as guilty as anyone. I folded down some pages I didn't want Carly to read. Plus a few for Lizabett, as well. And it was all because I was writing about men, first Randy and then Quinn.

I never thought any man would mess up the Sisterhood. But I'm beginning to wonder if it's happening now. What other reason would there be for so many secrets?

To make it even worse, I can't decide what to do about my date tonight with Randy. I wish I hadn't agreed to meet him for coffee. I wish I could keep this date a secret, but—despite all those folded pages—the Sisterhood has never been about secrets.

I'm tempted to find some excuse to cancel the date and not even tell anyone it was ever an option, but the Sisterhood has never been about cowardice, either.

I would call off my date tonight if Carly liked the grill guy. That would be a good, acceptable reason to cancel it—at least in my mind—I would tell Randy I couldn't get away from the diner.

But, from her remarks yesterday at the ball game, I don't think Carly likes him. Not in that way. She wouldn't complain the way she did about a man she liked. Even if she was angry at him, she would be silently loyal. That's the way Carly has been as long as I have known her.

Becca, now—well, Becca is a different story, and if she had spent any time at all with Randy, I would worry about her feelings. But she's so caught up in that internship, I don't think she's given the grill guy a second thought.

And Lizabett—well, no, I can't see Lizabett worrying about the grill guy.

Which pretty much means the only one who will be troubled if I go out with the grill guy is me. And I guess there's no point in keeping a secret from myself.

So in the spirit of openness, I am going to e-mail the Sisterhood and tell them about my date. I spent months whining about the grill guy when we first started knitting, and they deserve to know I'm finally having my date.

The earth should be shifting on its axis. But it's not.

I guess my problem is that I just thought the whole thing would be more fun. I always thought that, if I had been able to go out with the grill guy, the whole evening would have been gold-dusted romance and my heart would have been permanently altered. I thought that date would be a turning point in my life.

It doesn't feel that way anymore. I'd just as soon stay here and write in the journal or read a book or clear some tables. Maybe too much time has passed since I was hot for the grill guy—no pun intended, by the way. Maybe my enthusiasm just got worn down by waiting. Maybe—and I'm not willing to swear to this—the grill guy never was my dream guy after all.

Wow. Did I really write that down in black and white? Life is sometimes peculiar, isn't it?

As I've been standing here thinking and writing in the journal, I've been putting silver dangling earrings in my ears and fancy shoes on my feet. Lipstick colors my lips and my cheeks have a nice blush. I check myself in the mirror and I look good—ready for any date.

I wish I could dress my attitude up as easily as I prettied up the rest of me, but from where I stand now the best part of going out with Randy is that I will be able to chalk one up for my Sisterhood goal.

Speaking of which, I better send that e-mail.

I sit down at my computer and begin to

type. I keep it short: Goal in process. Coffee with the grill guy tonight. It will be date number one. That leaves 4 more days for 2 more dates. Looking for a busboy for date #2. Wish me luck.

I know that's going to get some reactions about my counting, but I have decided not to count any of my times with Quinn. I'm confused about how many dates, if any, we've had, and I refuse to count them anyway. I don't want to look at him as just a number on the way to meeting my goal. Quinn's my friend. He deserves better than to be a notch on some dating belt.

Of course, I suppose Randy does, too. Now, that's a thought to depress me. Since when have I, Marilee Davidson, been a user? And with the grill guy? What's my world coming to?

I put my jacket on and walk to the door of my office. Maybe Randy will want to make it an early night, too. I walk out into the main part of The Pews. Uncle Lou already knows where I'm going, so he waves at me from the counter. "Just make sure he walks you back here if it's late."

Uncle Lou doesn't want me walking down Colorado Boulevard alone after nine o'clock. Before that time, all of the businesses are open. Around nine a few start to close down and then more follow.

"I won't be that long," I say as I start moving toward the door.

I walk halfway to the door before I turn around. "There's a lot of people here to-night," I say to Uncle Lou. "Maybe I should cancel this coffee thing and help Annie wait tables. I can call Randy on his cell phone."

"There's no more people than usual. We'll do fine."

"I'll come back early," I say as I walk toward the door of The Pews.

"No need. Have some fun."

Yeah.

Colorado Boulevard is lit up at night. There are restaurants and little boutiques all of the way up and down the street. Half of the restaurants have outside seating so the sound of people laughing and having a good time spreads over the whole street. It feels good just to be outside hearing it all. Someone is playing a saxophone in one of the restaurants and the sound pours out onto the street. I think I can even see a few stars—or maybe it's just the lights on top of Mount Wilson.

Randy is waiting for me at the coffee place. I notice him right away. I've got eyes. I can see he's looking fine. His black shirt makes his stormy gaze look deeper and more mysterious and brooding than ever. There's a blond woman sitting alone at the counter, and she is just waiting to see if someone joins him. I know. I see her scowling at me as I walk toward his table.

Okay, this is it, I tell myself as I wait for something to click inside me. Maybe I was slow to get excited, but this is the real thing. There's still no click. I suddenly begin to worry about what I will say to this man while we drink our coffee. And how long do we need to sit here? Is an hour long enough for a coffee date?

I sit down.

I hope I'm going to have fun writing all of this down for you later, because a closer look at Randy's face tells me neither one of us is going to have loads of fun tonight.

At least the coffee will be strong. I order

a Colombian blend when someone asks me what I want.

I love the smells of all of the coffees and the place is full of windows and plants. I mention that one of the plants is a particularly fine-looking philodendron. Randy nods in agreement.

Our first twenty minutes are pathetic. We are reduced to actually talking about the coffee. Does anyone really do that? You know, listing the benefits of freshly ground beans and wondering if certain flavors add or detract from a good cup of coffee. We could be a commercial for coffee—and not one of those glamorous commercials with the attractive people sipping coffee before beginning their exciting days.

No, we are more like an ad for some cable station that can't afford actors so they use someone's cousins who don't know what to say and there's nothing extra for a stage or makeup or even a really good cup of coffee for inspiration.

You don't want to be there.

Once we finish talking about coffee, Randy begins to relax. Then he starts to complain about Carly and how she is the most confusing woman he's ever met and how she runs hot and cold and every temperature in between.

"Carly?" I say at the last bit. The Carly I know is more even-tempered than anyone I've ever met. She never snaps or yells or confuses people. "You mean our Carly?"

"Yeah," the grill guy says, and he broods some more.

I take another sip of my coffee. Humm, this is interesting.

"Maybe she's coming down with something," I finally say, to give Randy some comfort. The guy looks miserable.

"Yeah?" Randy perks up at this. "Do you think that's why she wouldn't go out with me?"

"I don't know. When did you ask her out?"

"Yesterday morning—before we went over to the ball game," Randy says. "Maybe it's my timing."

Now who's keeping secrets? I think to myself. Carly hasn't said a word. This adds a whole new light on Carly's attitude at the game. Maybe I didn't read her emotions as well as I thought I had.

"I asked her to go to dinner in the Ritz-

Carlton Dining Room," Randy continues. "I thought she'd like the place—it's classy and all. Stuffed lobster and atmosphere—that kind of thing. I even called to make reservations. Of course, I had to cancel them later, but..."

I am starting to feel a little stirring of emotion finally. "Did you ask her for tonight?"

Randy nods.

I don't know why that should annoy me, but it does. Carly got an invitation to dinner at the Ritz-Carlton, and I got a cup of coffee. "Maybe she'll change her mind."

Randy shakes his head. "All she thinks about is that cat of hers."

I try to hold on to my indignation about the dinner versus the cup of coffee, but I find I can't. Randy looks too pathetic, and Carly will be so excited. "She is a wonderful person. You wouldn't want to let her get away."

Randy looks at me oddly. "She said the same thing about you."

"She did?" For the first time since I've stepped into the coffee place, I feel a genuine smile curling my lips. "Isn't that nice of her?"

I can always count on the Sisterhood.

"Yeah, real nice," Randy says as he takes another gulp of coffee. He sets his cup down.

I am feeling pretty good about now. "I think if you ask Carly out again, she might say yes."

"Really?" Randy is looking interested now.

I nod.

"I thought maybe I'm not rich enough for her," Randy finally says. "You saw that house."

"Oh, yeah." I didn't add that I even counted the chandeliers. And noticed the maid with the uniform. And did a quick appraisal of the value of all that land in the heart of one of the most expensive neighborhoods in all of Los Angeles County.

"I grew up in Fontana," Randy says. "Nobody has a house like that out there."

"No, I suppose not."

I can see Randy is working his way through his fears.

"Carly's not a snob," I say. "She's reserved, but she's not all about money."

Randy nods.

"Maybe next time just ask her to meet you for coffee," I say. "Start out a little smaller. Don't put so much pressure on both of you."

I know I sound a little like Dear Abby, but that's the way I'm feeling so I go with it.

By now Randy is grinning wide enough to make the woman at the counter look at me as though she's wondering what my secret is. I just smile at her. Who knew I had it in me to bring a look like that to the grill guy's face? The woman at the counter doesn't need to know the look is courtesy of good advice.

When I get back to The Pews, I come right back to my office so I can write about it all in this journal. I can't believe I waited six years for this date.

The only good part of the date was the realization that Randy isn't interested in me any more than I am interested in him. Well, that and the fact that I am genuinely one hundred percent happy for Carly. I can't wait for her to tell us about Randy. We'll have to devote a whole tab in the journal to that. Actually, we don't have any tabbed sections yet, but I think this might warrant one—a large one. Maybe it should even be volume two of this journal thing. That'd be nice. Carly could be in charge of that one.

I help Uncle Lou lockup that night.

Lockup is my favorite time of the day and I stay whenever I can. Uncle Lou seems happier than usual tonight. Maybe there is something in the air around here besides smog tonight.

"It's good to see you go out," he says to me as he puts clean glasses in the rack over the counter. He does that every night. "A young woman like you should have a boyfriend."

"I don't need a boyfriend to be happy," I say as I wipe down the counter. I have already completely closed the window blinds.

"You're too serious," Uncle Lou says. "A boyfriend might make you laugh more."

I shrug and keep wiping. "I laugh enough."

"Not everyone is like your parents," Uncle Lou says. He finishes with the glasses and starts untying the apron he wears. "Always fighting. Some marriages are about laughing, too."

Uncle Lou walks me to my car in the parking structure even though he lives in a small apartment over the diner so this means he has to walk back to his place afterward. Whenever he does this, he says it's good to stretch his legs.

When we get to my car, I give Uncle Lou another hug good-night. His legs have been stretched all day long; he's not walking me to the parking place because he wants some exercise. "You're the best."

Uncle Lou hugs me back, "You're not so bad yourself."

Yeah, I definitely have to hug my Uncle Lou more.

I think about Uncle Lou's words as I get ready to go to bed. When I slide into bed, I pull the covers up to my shoulders. The night is chilly enough that I want blankets on my bed.

I don't want to think about Uncle Lou's words, but I do. I wonder if he's right. Did my parents' marriage lower my expectations for finding happiness with a man? I had always assumed it was the cancer that did that—especially when I had the partial mastectomy. Despite what I told the others earlier, I do feel a little different about my body now. Not hugely, horribly different. It is just that I never take my body for granted the way I did before. I'm not sure what that means for me and men.

I worry when I wear T-shirts that they

might be too tight even if they are modest. The reconstruction on my breast had gone very well, but I have yet to put on a swimsuit that isn't matronly.

If a man hugs me—and only a few have since my operation—I always turn to the side a little. Of course, it might be my father who's responsible for that. He stopped giving me regular hugs when he left Mom and me. If he hugs me at all now, it's an arm around the shoulders kind of half hug. It could be the partial mastectomy or it could be because of his leaving that he does that.

I go to sleep wondering if my cancer will follow me all of my life, or if the day will ever come when it will be as if I'd never had it.

Chapter Twelve

Do not employ handsome servants.
—Chinese proverb

Sometimes we just couldn't take another serious thought. That's when someone, usually Rose, would bring us a silly quote and we would sit and talk about what our lives might have been. When Rose brought us the handsome servant quote, Lizabett thought we should pretend to have servants.

It was Becca who pointed out that we already did have servants—well, sort of.

We spent weeks chuckling over our handsome servants—the nurses, the lab techs, the doctors—all of them working for us. The whole thing wasn't much, but I can't tell you what it did for us to have our own private joke that no one else understood.

I wonder if someone in a thousand years will pick through the pages of our journal and find little proverbs or quotes. By that time, cancer will hopefully be a novelty and the idea of us sharing our thoughts about the disease might interest people. We'll be like the old Chinese people who wrote the proverbs I've used in this journal. If these pages get that ancient, I want to say right up front that anyone is welcome to quote anything in them. And don't bother to try and figure out which one of us wrote the words you pick. Anonymous is fine with us.

I hope you can read my writing okay. I haven't exactly written things down with a thought to preserving them that long. Anyway, if you can't make out a word or two just make up one that sounds as if it fits. Don't worry if it's the wrong word. We'll all be gone by then so we won't care.

I woke up feeling determined. I don't know what I had been thinking about during the night—whether it was my Uncle Lou's words or the realization that I had faced my fears and my dreams both when I went out with the grill guy after so many years—but sometime during the night I decided I was tired of hiding from my fears and hopes. Hopes are sometimes just fears flipped around, don't you think? It seemed that way to me this morning as I lay in my bed and watched the sunshine work its way through the blinds in my bedroom.

Anyway, I decided to talk to my father. Today, after work, I will go to his apartment and, in a very civilized manner, I will ask him if he knew I had cancer when he left me there with Mom. Just like that. I'll put the question out there.

I am writing this all down in the journal so that I won't back out. I'm not going to fold any pages over or put in any clips. Everyone is free to read what I am going to do. And, if I haven't done it, they are welcome to nag me until I do.

I know the other day at The Pews my father probably overheard my conversation with Uncle Lou, but I need to know for sure.

I need to hear from his own lips that he left us knowing I was sick.

I don't know what I will do with that knowledge. I don't think I'll be ready to forgive my father if he did know about my cancer when he left and I'm not sure I'll believe him if he claims he didn't know. It's one of those no-win situations.

I could always ask Pastor Engstrom about it all when I go to his group on Thursday morning—and I intend to go. There's a lot I don't know about things like forgiveness and faith. I'm beginning to think Quinn is right about it not being easy. Plus, now that my father knows I've gone to church, it doesn't feel as though it's so complicated to go again. He never once seemed to think I was taking sides.

In the meantime, I want to spend some of my time today calling around to see if I can find a place for Lizabett's ballet troupe to have their performance. I go into The Pews around ten and I usually have some time before lunch when I can do some calling.

I'm also going to check my e-mail and see if I have any responses to my announcement about my date with the grill guy. I am especially interested in what Carly's response will be, if anything. I might even invite everyone over to The Pews for lunch today. It's a long time until Thursday, and I think we might need to touch base with each other. I particularly want to give Carly the message that the grill guy is all hers—which isn't something you can just blurt out in an e-mail. It requires some finesse.

I drive down Foothill Boulevard and then go south to Colorado Boulevard to get to The Pews. If there's no roadwork going on, it's an easy drive. Today I have to wait for a couple of trucks beside a construction site—new condos going up. But I don't mind the wait. It's a warm day and I can see the leaves starting to come back on those trees that lose their leaves around here, which is not all of them.

The Pews is never busy on Monday morning, and once I greet everyone, there's no need for my help up front, so I head back to my office.

I don't even get back to my office before I hear Becca coming in the door and saying hello to Uncle Lou. I wait in the hallway going to my office because I can hear footsteps.

"There you are," Becca says as she turns the corner and sees me.

I think she's here to talk about me counting my dates, but she's not.

"I need a job," Becca says as she walks closer. "Well, I guess it shouldn't be a job—at least I shouldn't get paid."

"You want to work for free?"

Becca nods. She's walking toward my office and, since she's not stopping where I am in the hall, I follow her to my office door. I keep my door locked so I get the key out of my purse and open the door.

Becca turns the light on as she steps through the door and heads for my spare chair next to the desk. "I talked to that law clerk finally. Seven o'clock this morning I called. I knew someone like him would be at his desk before everyone else."

Becca seems very satisfied with herself.

"Sounds like a guy with no life." I walk over to my desk and set down my purse.

"I think I got to him before he really woke up." Becca grins as she settles into my guest chair. "He complained he hadn't even had his coffee."

"So what did he say?" I sit down myself.

"He said I'm not well-rounded. That's why I didn't get the internship. I don't volunteer any place."

"Doesn't he know you've been sick?" I say.

"That's just it," Becca says with another grin. "They don't care if I've been sick. Turns out they have a formula and everyone gets so many points for each thing—grades, references, community involvement—that kind of thing."

"Well, so they're not discriminating against you."

Becca shakes her head. "It's all done by points. They didn't care about my religion or my health status. Just those points."

I look at Becca for any signs of strain. "You seem to be taking it well."

"This guy—the law clerk—he told me about another internship with a federal judge at the courthouse downtown. Said I would enjoy that one even more and no one hardly even knows about that one, so they don't have many applications. He's friends with the law clerk who handles it."

"Well, that's good."

"I'm going to apply today."

I silently count the number of days between today and this Thursday. It's a maximum of four. "How long will it take to find out if you get it?"

I can see by the look on Becca's face she hasn't realized until now what the delay will mean. "I'm not going to make my goal."

"It's not a big deal. So you meet it in a few weeks instead of Thursday."

"I've never given up on a goal." Becca's face is pale. "I've never done that."

"Maybe we need to all give ourselves more time to meet our goals," I say. I am certainly hoping for more time.

Becca looks at me as if I've suggested we not pay our taxes.

I hear footsteps coming down the hall fast and I look up just as Lizabett reaches my doorway. She's breathing hard and her hair is flying around her face which means she took off a scarf recently.

"Maybe we can at least help Lizabett reach her goal," I say to Becca, assuming that's why Lizabett is looking so harried. "You might even consider volunteering to help the ballet studio."

Lizabett starts talking when she hits my doorway and looks right at me. "You had your date with the grill guy." She doesn't look thrilled about it. "Date number one."

I nod.

"Well, that's just fine," Lizabett says as she steps inside my office. "I hope you wrote about it in the journal."

I nod.

"Well, I have something to write in the journal, too," Lizabett says.

I have never seen Lizabett this assertive. She looks positively fierce.

"Did my dad talk to you?" I ask, thinking maybe he has told her that he couldn't find a place for the ballet.

"I'm going to write about it first," Lizabett says stubbornly. "Some things are just better written in the journal."

I reach over and pick up the journal. "Here."

Lizabett takes the journal. "I'll be out front writing."

"Whew," Becca says when Lizabett is gone. "I wonder what she's so mad about."

"Probably her ballet," I say as I pick up my phone. "I should take some time to make some calls."

"I should go tell her I'm volunteering to help, too," Becca said as she stood.

"Oh, can you stay for lunch today?" I ask. "I thought I'd try to get everyone together and since you and Lizabett are already here, I'll call Carly and see if she can drive over."

"Sounds good," Becca says as she walks toward the door. "Hopefully, by that time we'll know where the ballet will be."

I nod. In the meantime, I wonder what Lizabett is writing in the journal. I also wonder if she will take the time to read what I've already written this morning about my father.

Hi, this is Lizabett. I need to write this down some place so that I don't say it aloud. I am stupid, stupid, stupid. I guess I really sort of thought that Quinn was taking Marilee out as a favor to me—I mean, he does everything he can for me. I thought he was worried about all of the Sisterhood meeting their goals and that he was just being nice and taking Marilee on a few dates so she would meet hers, too.

Of course, I knew he liked her, but I didn't know he *liked* her. And there I was this morning, running off my mouth about

Marilee having a date with the grill guy—which didn't seem to surprise Quinn—but then he asked how many dates this made for her meeting her goals, and I said she had said it was one.

I didn't even think about what I was saying—I mean, that's what Marilee had said in her e-mail. I didn't realize Quinn might take it the wrong way. I'm sure his dates were perfectly nice dates even if Marilee isn't counting them.

Oh, dear, what am I to do? I know you're only a journal and you can't answer me back, but I could use some help. I'm writing this fast, because I see Becca and Marilee walking this way.

I don't know why we need to have these goals anyway. Nobody is meeting them.

I'm going to fold this page down and then give the journal back to Marilee. When I get it all folded down, I think I will stick it together with some tape. Quinn would not be happy with me if I let Marilee know his feelings are hurt. Quinn never wants anyone to worry about him.

I know I complain about him, but he's my big brother and I love him. If Marilee is so stuck on the grill guy that she can't see what a great guy Quinn is, then she's not the woman I thought she was. I guess I shouldn't say that, either. Oh, well, I'm done now.

It took me—Marilee—a good fifteen minutes to get the journal back. Lizabett wouldn't let me have it until she borrowed some masking tape from Uncle Lou and taped her page so tightly shut that I don't know if it will ever open up for reading. Remember what I said earlier about the people years from now who might want to read this journal—well, if that happens—I'm sorry about the pages and I hope you have something that removes tape from paper by then.

Anyway, I'm not as worried about the tape issue as I am about Lizabett. Something is wrong, but she won't say what it is. She has put her black scarf on, however, and she's sitting on a hard chair near one of the rear tables looking like a recent immigrant with an attitude.

"I'm going to call City Hall," I say to Lizabett. Becca has already gone to call her law clerk to see if volunteering to help with the ballet would count on her application. "They let groups use their courtyard in the evenings. I think it's marble and would work just fine for ballet. We could put folding chairs up around the edge of the courtyard and you'd be all set."

Lizabett nods in one swift bobbing motion. "That would be okay."

It doesn't take a genius to tell something is bothering Lizabett. "Maybe we could even put up some pink balloons around to make it look more festive. Or red ones. The color doesn't matter."

Lizabett nods again. This time she crosses her arms, too. "Is the grill guy going to help with the chairs?"

"Well, maybe."

"He's kind of skinny. My brothers should help, too."

"Well, we'll have everything set up in no time at all—no matter where we find a place for the performance," I say.

"A chair's nothing to my brother Quinn. He can lift anything. I bet he's stronger than the grill guy."

"Most men can lift a folding chair." I am anxious to stop all of this talk about how skinny or strong the grill guy is, because I see that Carly has just come in the diner door and I don't want her to think that we've been talking about Randy—which I guess we have, but not for any good reason that I can see.

"Carly," I say. "I was just going to call and ask if you're free for lunch in a couple of hours."

"That works," Carly said. "I just came down here to give you an update on my cat."

"Oh?"

Carly gave a nod. "Marie came in this morning. She's in my room now."

"Well, that's good news," I say, even though Carly doesn't look particularly happy. "Was everything all right?"

Carly looks at me blankly.

"With your cat," I add. "Was everything all right with your cat?"

Carly nods and then frowns. "Your grill guy put one of those boxes at the bottom of the tree yesterday before we went to the ball game. I told him not to, but I guess he did anyway. The gardener found Marie in it this morning and, when he let her out in the house, she came straight for the room outside my bedroom. That's where I keep her dish."

"She must have been hungry."

"She didn't eat the tuna in that box thing. Your grill guy didn't know what he was talking about."

"He's not my grill guy," I say. "In fact, I think you and he would make a good couple."

I'm not sure Carly is even listening to me. She's already turned to walk back out the door. "You'll have to tell me the details of your big date when I get back. Right now, I have to go get a leash for my cat."

"It wasn't so much a date," I call after Carly, but she doesn't stop to listen.

I've never seen Carly walk away when someone is talking to her. She's much too polite to do that even if she is bored. What do you suppose it is all about? If you're thinking what I'm thinking, there can only be one explanation. Carly seriously likes the grill guy. Which is good news—I think.

Chapter Thirteen

...if I ever go looking for my heart's desire again, I won't look any further than my own backyard...

—Judy Garland as Dorothy in *The Wizard of Oz*

Lizabett was the one who wanted us all to talk about our hearts' desires one night while we were knitting. You might have noticed we spent a lot of time that first year in the Sisterhood talking about our dreams. Some days it seemed as though our dreams were all we had to hold on to. Our present was troubled. Our past was over. So we had our dreams.

This was the first time that we tried to find our hearts' desires in our backyards. We took that to mean in our homes. We all looked so bleak you wouldn't know we were talking about our hearts' desires if you looked at our faces and didn't listen to our words.

I, of course, wished for my dad back. I even got the words out. Lizabett wished for her freedom from her brothers. Neither Carly nor Becca would share their hearts' desires, although I only had to look at their faces to know that they each had one. I guess all of our homes were a little troubled in those days.

It takes me a couple of minutes to realize what Carly said on her way out the door of The Pews. "She's going to get a leash for her cat? *Carly?*"

Lizabett looks up at that. "She would never put her cat on a leash. She didn't even want to use that box thing to trap her cat. And the cat would only be in there eating a can of tuna."

"I know," I say. At least, I think I know that. Things have been so weird lately, I don't know what's what for sure anymore.

Becca has come back from her phone call and hears what I've said. "Maybe it's because of the picture in the paper."

Both Lizabett and I look at Becca.

"I haven't seen it," she says. "But the law clerk and I were talking and he told me about it. It's in the *Star News* this morning. A picture of Carly looking for her cat."

I have a bad feeling about this, and I rush outside to look in the newspaper stands outside the diner. Both Lizabett and Becca are right behind me until we reach the newspapers, and then we all just stand there and stare.

"It's on the front page," Lizabett says in awe. "In color."

"Uh-huh," I say as I dig in my pocket for a couple of quarters.

The picture is sharp and clear, so there is no mistaking Carly for someone else. Of course, the paper only used the picture because Carly is beautiful. I bet they sell more papers today than usual. Who wouldn't want to look at one of the beautiful people?

The sky is blue, and Carly is looking up into the trees with her house in the background, including the maid and cook standing on the steps. The caption reads San Marino Cat Chooses Tree House Over Mansion As Owner Answers Charges About Contaminants.

"Her hair looks good," Becca says as I reach over and open the box that lets you pull a paper from the stand.

"Carly always looks beautiful," I say as I pick up a newspaper. "That doesn't mean they have to plaster her picture all over town."

Carly is too private to enjoy this.

"I don't think it's fair to call your uncle's bacon strips 'contaminants,' though," Becca adds thoughtfully. "They are a bit hard on the arteries maybe, but contaminants is going too far."

At least the story doesn't say where Carly got the bacon. No one would want the diner mentioned in the same headline as contaminants.

"Does it mention Quinn?" Lizabett asks before leaning closer to me. "Quinn ate some of that bacon, you know. He always takes a good picture. They should have gotten him in there, too, eating a slice of that bacon."

"I'm not sure anyone wants their picture in a newspaper with this kind of a headline," I say as I hold up the paper so everyone can see the picture, caption and the headline. At least they didn't mention that the police wanted to give us all tickets for littering. They didn't give us tickets, by the way—I'm not sure I told you that earlier.

"What else does it say?" Becca asks.

I read the caption to them:

"Local woman, Carly Winston, 24, tries to lure runaway cat home by leaving fried bacon on the street outside her parent's San Marino mansion. Winston claims the cat, a purebred animal, didn't mean to run away from home, but is merely confused because it is a new San Marino resident. Will the smell of bacon bring the cat home? Winston purchased the cat recently for an undisclosed sum of money from a cat breeder in Washington State."

Becca whistles. "That makes Carly sound like she's up to no good—saying things like 'undisclosed sum of money'—it's no one's business how much Carly paid for that cat."

"People in San Marino spend their money like water anyway," Lizabett says. "So, they should talk."

We all turn to go back inside The Pews.

"Yeah, I know, but those people in San Marino think it's in bad taste to mention the word money in a newspaper," I say. "They all like to pretend money doesn't matter."

We're inside the door of The Pews now, but Lizabett and I are still looking at that newspaper. Becca goes over to the counter to talk to Uncle Lou.

"Quinn has a savings account," Lizabett says after a bit. "A good-sized one, too. And he's not squeamish about it—I mean, they could mention it in the paper if they wanted and he'd be okay with it. He's cool about money."

Our eyes adjust to being inside The Pews. The light was bright outside, but the blinds are half-closed and it's dim inside here.

"That reminds me," I say. "I need to call City Hall and find out how much it costs to rent their courtyard."

"Did your dad ask about us using the car dealership place yet?" Lizabett asks.

I shake my head. I've been dreading this question. "I haven't talked to him today."

"Do you think you'll call him?" Lizabett asks.

I don't know what to tell Lizabett. The truth of the matter is that I can't call my father because I don't have his telephone number. Uncle Lou has the number, and I could always get it from him, but I don't.

"I thought I'd walk over to the car dealership," I finally say. It is several blocks from here, across the Colorado Bridge, and it's close enough to make a nice walk. My dad will be surprised to see me walk in the dealership door, but he would be just as surprised if I called him later. Besides, he won't be home until this evening, so if I want a quick answer, it's best to go to the dealership.

The door opens to The Pews, and I see a huge bouquet of long-stemmed red roses come inside. I can see the khaki legs of a deliveryman at the bottom of the bouquet and a hunk of black hair at the top. I don't need to read the card to know what is happening. There's got to be two dozen roses there.

"They're from Randy," I say.

Obviously, the guy did not take my advice about starting a little more low-key with Carly. And, who knows, maybe he's right. Red roses and Carly do go together. At least red roses go with her better than cat leashes do.

"Put them over there," I tell the delivery guy as I gesture to one of the back tables. I reach in my pockets and pull out a few one-dollar bills to tip the guy. The deliveryman takes the tip and heads over to the back table with the flowers.

"Well," Lizabett says as if she's going to say something and then pauses for so long I think she's lost her words. But she hasn't. "They're only flowers. Quinn can send flowers, too."

I don't know what to say to Lizabett, but it turns out I don't need to say anything because she walks into a corner and pulls out her cell phone. I can't hear what she's saying, but whatever it is, she's saying it with a force that is new to Lizabett.

Becca walks back over to me. She's noticed the animation in Lizabett's voice, too. "Would you listen to that?"

Neither one of us can actually hear the words Lizabett is saying, but we both recognize the tone. Lizabett is taking charge.

"I hope she's calling Carly," I finally say. "I don't know where Carly thinks she's going to find a cat leash here in Old Town anyway, so she might as well come back and take care of her flowers."

You can find many things in the stores around The Pews. Carly can find Italian walking shoes if she wants or twenty flavors of gelato—Italian ice cream—or silk scarves in a hundred colors or hand-dipped candles, but she won't find something as mundane as a cat leash.

"I might go and call Carly myself," Becca says. "To make sure she keeps that cat in her room until after Thursday. Leash or no leash, we need to be sure one of us meets our goal."

"I should go make some calls myself," I say as I start to walk toward my office. I want to have some alternatives to mention to Lizabett when I break the news to her that the dealership isn't available. "Hang around for lunch, though—when Carly gets back, we can eat."

I take some time when I am back in my office to write a full account of everything that's been happening in this journal. Of course, I start with my decision to walk over to my dad's car dealership after lunch. What do you think of that? I used to visit him there once in a while before everything changed. I always liked the smells—I don't know if it's the new leather or just the new cars themselves—but whatever it is, I like it. It's a Cadillac dealership by the way so they keep the place sparkling.

My dad is good at his job, too. He's been working as the accountant at this same place for over ten years now, and he's always winning employee of the month—I know because Uncle Lou tells me. Uncle Lou is proud of his little brother.

It's funny what shape a family takes—Uncle Lou has been more like a father to me in the past six years than my dad has been, and I don't know how either one of them feel about it. I'm my uncle's only niece, which is one of the reasons he invited me to go into the business with him. Years ago, we all used to celebrate holidays together—Uncle Lou would come over for dinner and we'd all eat and play board games. Those were fun times.

Of course, that all stopped with the big separation. My parents haven't gotten a divorce even though it's been six years ago now that my dad walked out. I know my mom doesn't want to file for a divorce. So she just left it for Dad, and I guess he's leaving it for her. It's almost funny—the same stubbornness that made Dad move out is the same stubbornness that's keeping them technically married.

Meanwhile, we're all in limbo—not going forward but not sliding backward either.

I shake myself. I don't need to be worrying about the status of my parent's marriage when I go to see my father. I will be doing well just to get my question asked about using the showroom for Lizabett's ballet program. An added bonus in going to talk to my dad at his work is that I can see the showroom floor for myself. The room I remember would work well for a ballet performance, but changes might have been made over the past six years.

As you and I both know, a lot can change in that time.

Well, will you look at that? The pen that I have been using to write in the journal is running out of ink. I'll have to take a break and search my desk drawer for another small one like the one I'm using. I like it because it has a fine black point. I always think a fine point like that makes a journal look classy although, if you could see the folded pages and the tape and the clips, you would know that being classy is something we gave up on a while back in this endeavor.

I look up at the clock before I start my phone calling. It is fifteen minutes past eleven in the morning. When Carly gets back, we'll be able to eat lunch. I hope she's talking to me by then. If nothing else, the flowers should put her in a forgiving mood.

It takes me a few minutes to call City Hall, and the woman I talk to tells me this Wednesday evening is open for a private party, but that there's a problem if the ballet troupe is charging admission. I hadn't thought of that. Of course, they will have to refund the money for the tickets if they don't give a performance at all so maybe they'd want to do the ballet for free to the fifty or so people who were planning to attend.

At least it gives me one option for Lizabett. I'm hoping we will find a place for the ballet because I'd like to see Lizabett dance. Lizabett has always been a little shy, but she's never lacked in passionate emotions. I know that seems strange, but sometimes you can just see the emotions playing on her face—anger, indignation, sympathy—you can see them all even though she seldom speaks. I think Lizabett has more in common with her brothers than she thinks.

I smile a little. Quinn has a nice face to read, too. I'd like to watch his face as Lizabett dances.

Oh, I hear Carly talking.

"Did you see your flowers?" I say as the door to my office opens and Carly stands there. "I'm assuming Randy sent them for you."

"Don't be silly," Carly says. "I sent them here myself."

"You sent them? Who to? No, forget I asked." I figure maybe I'm too behind the times in dating. Do you suppose Carly got Randy flowers?

Carly doesn't answer my question anyway. "Is that the journal over there? I need to write something in it."

I nod. I am still stunned that Carly sent the flowers. "Are they for Lizabett? The flowers?"

Carly shakes her head. "They're for my aunt—to say I'm sorry."

"What'd you do?"

"The unforgivable."

By this time, Carly has bent her head over the pages of the journal so I figure I should leave and put in my order for lunch. "Is the shrimp Caesar salad good for you for lunch?"

Carly looks up and nods. "Dressing on the side."

"I know," I say as I close the door to my office.

Hi, this is Carly. You will not believe what I have done. I can't tell the Sisterhood about it because they believe the caption they read in the *Star News* is true. I've never told them that my parents and I live with my aunt and uncle. I'm so used to keeping that little fact private that I never thought about what might happen if I didn't clarify the situation to that reporter.

The truth is I'm a little ashamed of the way my parents and I live with my aunt and uncle, so I try not to even admit it to myself. I mean we don't even pay rent or anything. In fact, my uncle even gives my mom an allowance for groceries. We are complete deadbeats.

But this picture in the paper is going to blow the lid off of everything.

My aunt was livid when she read that the paper says the house belongs to my parents. She is so proud of that house. Of course, we all know that she and my uncle own the house, but she worries about what the neighbors will think. And she's got a point. Some of the neighbors are nice, but those who came out when the police were there will believe any crazy thing they hear. And if they read it in the newspaper, well…

I don't know what to do, but I got my aunt flowers and I'm going to get a leash for my cat just as soon as I can find one. I won't use the leash with Marie while she's inside my rooms, but when I take her outside of my rooms and through the rest of the house, she will be on a leash.

I wonder if I can convince Marie the leash is a cat necklace. Maybe I'll get one that sparkles.

Anyway, that's all I have for now. I'm folding these pages back so no one else can read them. Thanks for listening. I find it always helps me think things through when I can write them down in this journal.

I'll keep you posted. For now, I'm going to go out and eat lunch with the Sisterhood.

Wait a minute—I just realized what I heard Marilee say about the flowers. She thought Randy was sending them *to me.* Oh, dear, I can't let that impression grow. Randy is wonderful and under different circumstances, but—well, there's no point in wishing for what can't be. He's not the man for me.

Or, should I say, I'm not the woman for him.

No matter. You understand.

Chapter Fourteen

Be not afraid of growing slowly,
Be afraid only of standing still.
—Chinese proverb

It was when we were recovering from our cancer and starting to feel better that we became most frustrated. Rose brought this quote to us during that time. I haven't said much about Rose in this journal, but I'm thinking we should dedicate the whole thing to her. Maybe we'll even get it typeset one of these days and present it to her like a plaque.

As you know, Rose was a student counselor at the hospital where she met all of us and it was her idea to start this group. She was very wise at the time, because she didn't pretend to know everything. She mostly just let us talk and talk. I think that's why she'd like this journal. It's just more of the talk she's heard for years from us.

Sometimes I wonder if we have any more answers today than we did back then. Rose would know. She's always the one who knew when we were going forward even if it was slowly.

None of us need to be served when we're in The Pews so we each just pick up our order and take it into the Sisterhood room. We call it that even though other people can use the room if it's not Thursday night. Today there's no one sitting in there until we enter—which is nice.

Carly brought the journal with her when she came out for lunch, and so this is Marilee back with her pen—well, technically, it's a different pen now, but you know what I mean.

We're all eating salads, so there's some talking as we see to our dressings. Some of us take vinegar and oil, some Thousand island, some French—the bottles all go around. In the middle of all this, Carly keeps asking me why I would even think Randy would send her roses when he had just gone out with me, and I keep saying something light—you know, that he's a nice guy and that kind of thing and maybe he was happy her cat was finally back home or he was sorry he had to use the box trap thing.

What *can* I say? I don't want to make Randy's move for him by telling Carly that he still hopes to go out with her. I was going to tell her earlier, but she's so agitated today I can't predict what she'll think about anything I say. I also don't want to say anything that might make her not want to go out with him.

The best thing to do, I decide, is to change the subject. Besides, even though Lizabett seems to be interested in the conversation about the roses and Randy, Becca sure isn't.

"It's called Feline Fancy," Becca is saying for the second time to Carly as Carly is muttering yet again that Randy should be sending me roses. Becca stabs at her salad and then presses on, "It's got different flavors. Ground-up fillet mignon for one, I think. And crabmeat or something exotic like that. Maybe liver pâté."

"For a cat?" Carly finally zeroes in on Becca's conversation. Carly's fork is suspended in midair. "I'm not so sure you'd give a cat liver pâté."

"If you want your cat to stay at home, maybe you do," Becca says as she forks another bite of salad. "A happy cat is a cat that stays where she's put."

"Marie is a very good cat," Carly says. She lays her fork down on her plate and looks at Becca fully. "She's just high-energy."

Becca nods, "Then she'll like Feline Fancy. The ads make it sound positively addictive."

Carly frowns but before she can say anything, I jump in.

"That's just a figure of speech," I say. "Becca just wants to be sure Marie will be there on Thursday so we can count her as a goal accomplished."

Carly's frown clears and she picks up her fork. "Of course, the goals."

This doesn't make Becca too happy. "Don't tell me you've forgotten the goals, too?"

"Of course not," Carly says.

"Me, neither," Lizabett adds.

I lift up my hands. "I'm trying."

"We're not going to make it," Becca mutters.

I don't think it's diplomatic to remind Becca that she might be the furthest of any of us from her goal—well, maybe she'd tied with me. I'm pretty far away from meeting my goal, too.

I'm thinking about this when the door to the Sisterhood opens and there stands Quinn in his full fireman uniform. His arms are full of frothy, sparkling wings.

"You brought them." Lizabett stands and greets him.

"I'm on my lunch hour, and I only have fifteen minutes left," Quinn says as he surveys the rest of us with a scowl on his face before turning back to Lizabett. "I don't know why you need your wings today anyway."

I have been smiling at Quinn since he appeared in the doorway, but my lips are growing a little stiff since he hasn't even nodded or said hello or anything. I must admit I am surprised that there's not a little bit of a hello for me considering everything.

"Would you like some lunch?" I offer as I stand. "I could make you something—a sandwich if you need to be quick."

"No, thanks," Quinn says as he finally looks at me. "I saw your roses. Must have been some date."

"Oh, the roses are Carly's," I say.

"Oh," Quinn says as he gives a quick look at Lizabett. "I didn't know that."

"Yes, they're mine," Carly says cheerfully from the table. "Bought them myself to give to my aunt."

"That's nice," Quinn says. He's looking a little puzzled. "Considerate."

"Necessary," Carly mutters.

"I did hear the date went well, though," Quinn says as he walks a step closer to me. "Congratulations."

"It was only coffee," I say.

Quinn shrugs. "At least it was good enough to earn a point. That's something. I hope you get the other two in before Thursday."

Quinn is not saying that in any friendly

way, so it's clear he's not offering to be any of those points. What he says next confirms it. "If you need a backup, my brother Gregory is off the next couple of days."

I nod. "Thanks."

Quinn leaves as quickly as he came, and the only evidence that he'd even been here is the wings Lizabett is holding.

"Are you practicing today?" I ask Lizabett.

She nods. "I guess I better."

Lizabett doesn't look any happier than me, but we both go back to our salads.

"He should have taken a sandwich," Lizabett finally says. "He'll get hungry."

Well, that's that, I say to myself as I take another fork of salad. Quinn is definitely cool toward me. Maybe he's worried I will make more of the times we've had coffee together than I should. Well, and maybe he's right—I certainly had been thinking we had something going on, and I'm clearly wrong.

You know what the worst thing about having cancer has been, well, apart from maybe dying? It's not knowing the things I'm supposed to know about things like dating.

I'm one of those people who got a late start at dating anyway. And then with my years of not dating because of the cancer, I feel as if I'm a whole decade behind where I should be in understanding the whole thing. I wish there were some remedial dating class I could take so I could figure it out.

My hunch is that the whole thing is twisted up with not understanding my father. Maybe I'm not expecting anything from men and so not getting anything. I'm sitting here eating my salad and thinking about the baseball caps I have back in my office.

Over the years, I've been so thrilled with those caps. Can you believe it? They're only baseball caps. They don't mean anything. They will never be enough to make up for what my father didn't give me—his care and concern when I was sick.

I'm not even listening to the others talk and eat their salads. I'm getting more and more upset. Finally, I decide I'm going to go over to that car dealership where my father is working right now and—and…well, at least I'm going to ask him about the use of the dealership for the ballet.

"Here," I give the journal back to Carly as I stand. "You keep this while I'm gone. I'm going to talk to my father."

I must have looked funny, because Lizabett says, "You don't need to—not if it's a problem."

"It's no problem," I say as I walk out the door of the Sisterhood room and into the main part of The Pews.

"I'm going to the dealership to see my father," I say loud enough for Uncle Lou to hear it behind the counter. "I won't be gone long."

I don't wait to hear if Uncle Lou has anything to say about my announcement. What can he say anyway? It is time for me to have a talk with my father. I don't care if I'm interrupting him and he's writing up the paperwork for the most expensive car on the lot. It's time for him to talk to me.

I march down Colorado Boulevard until I get past the bridge. Even then I don't slow much. It only takes me about ten minutes to reach the other side of the bridge. I see the dealership over by the Norton Simon museum. The dealership is mostly windows and there's a big swath of green grass in front of it. Some flowers are planted around the front of the building. Everything looks very upscale.

I, of course, go straight to the doors that enter into the main display floor. There's enough chrome and leather in the showroom to intimidate someone wearing blue jeans and a T-shirt. I suddenly realize I might feel more comfortable if I'd changed into something other than my work clothes. But it's too late now.

"I'd like to talk to Mr. Davidson," I say to the first man I meet. "He works here."

"I'd be happy to help you," the man starts to say and then smiles. "You're Marilee, aren't you?"

"Yes." I'm a little taken back at this.

"I'd know you anywhere," the man says. I look at him more closely to see if I recognize him from when I used to visit my dad here over six years ago. He doesn't look familiar.

"From your pictures," the man finally says. "Your dad has pictures of you in his office."

"Oh."

"I guess you don't know that your dad's been out sick today," the man continues.

Both the man and I look up when we hear my dad call out to me, "Marilee!"

My dad isn't wearing his usual working suit, and he looks a little pale.

"I heard you were coming, so I hurried over," my dad says as he walks over to us. "Don't worry. I'm not contagious. I sound like I have a cold, though, and I didn't want to scare customers off, so I stayed home this morning."

"Well, it was good meeting you, Marilee," the other man says as he turns to leave us.

"Yes, nice to meet you, too," I say to the man.

Then my father and I are standing there together, and neither one of us seems to know what to do.

"Well, why don't you come into my office?" my dad finally says. "Would you like any coffee or tea or anything?"

I shake my head. "I'm fine."

My dad has one of a row of offices at the back of the showroom.

"We usually meet with customers up front," my dad says as he opens the door so we can go inside. "I'm afraid this is just where I do my accounting."

I'm glad we're going to have some privacy.

My dad's office has a wooden desk with a computer on top. To the side are shelves filled with books. In front of the books are some pictures of me taken years ago.

"I'm surprised Mike recognized you from them," my dad says as he nods toward the pictures. "The last one I have is the one from your high school graduation."

I glance over at the pictures. He also has one of me as a baby and one that looks as though I was about ten years old.

"I didn't know you'd have pictures of me here," I say. He hadn't had pictures on his bookcase the last time I'd been here. As I recall, he had some plaques related to work.

"Well, I like to see you around when I'm working," my dad says with a pause. Neither one of us sits down. "I was going to call Lou later today and tell him that I talked to the general manager and asked about the ballet thing—he said it would be fine as long as it's after closing—which is seven that night."

"Really? Thanks."

"I'm happy to do it," my dad says. "I'll have

the key for closing. If your friends can take care of folding chairs, I'll ask the guys to move the show cars out to the lot for the night."

I feel a little awkward now that my dad's doing me a favor, so I step a little closer to look at the pictures of me. That's when I notice that there are three or four books on the corner of one of the shelves that have bright pink spines. All breast cancer patients know that color of pink. It's our color.

"What are these?" I say even though it is clear what they are. They are books on dealing with cancer. I reach for one and pull it off the shelf.

"Oh, those," my dad says as he sits on the corner of his desk. "I forgot they were there."

"Did you read them?" I look at the book and see it's title is *Coping with Cancer.*

"How else could I know what you were going through?" my dad says.

I close my eyes. "You could have asked me. We could have talked about it."

When I open my eyes, I know there are tears. "I really would have liked to talk to you about it."

There is a moment of silence.

"I didn't know what to say," my dad finally says.

I take a breath. It's now or never. "Is that why you left us—because of my cancer?"

My dad takes in a breath so quick it almost sounds like a hiss. "Of course not."

I nod. Okay, I can accept that. "But did you know I had cancer when you left?"

My dad is silent at that for a minute. "I thought you and your mother would be better off without me there."

"How can you say that?" I'm blinking now, but I'm not going to cry.

"I thought it was best for you. I didn't know how to stop arguing with your mom, and I knew that wasn't good for you when you were so sick."

"Couldn't you have tried?"

"I did try."

"You could have tried harder."

My dad nods. He looks sad. "There were times when I wished I had tried harder."

"I needed you."

"I know you did."

"Mom's not that hard to live with."

My dad smiled at that. "Maybe not—maybe it's me that's hard to live with."

I smile a little, too. "If it was the church thing that got to you—you need to know I'm going to church now. I mean, I just started, but I want to find out what it's all about."

My dad nods. "Is it because of that guy you met—what's his name—Quinn?"

I shrug. "It's Mom, too. She really believes it all."

My dad is silent at that. I don't think he gets it. I'm not sure I do, either, but I've decided to figure it all out.

"I've been worried you'll be mad if I go to church," I say. "Like I'm chosing Mom's side over yours."

"There are no sides," he says. "And maybe some Sunday I'll come with you."

I nod. Maybe he will, maybe he won't. I won't know until it happens so there's only one thing left to do. "Can I have a big bear hug?"

My dad looks relieved as he takes a step closer. "That I can do."

My dad puts his arm around my shoulder and gives me a squeeze.

I turn slightly so I'm facing him. "No, a real hug."

My dad folds me in his arms. "Like this?"

I nod my head.

"I'm always so afraid of hurting you. I don't want to hurt you."

"You can't hurt me with a hug."

My dad has his car with him so he gives me a ride back to The Pews before he goes back to his apartment. Before I leave his car, he scribbles his home telephone number on the back of his business card and says, "Call me at either place."

I nod. "I will."

I will, too. When I get out of my dad's car, I stand for a little bit in front of The Pews before I go inside. I know then that I'm going to write all of this down in the journal and that I should have something wise or moving to say about all that has happened. But I don't have anything articulate. Some of my anger about my dad is gone. I'm not sure, but I think some of my feelings about God have changed, too. All I know is that I feel a melting inside me of some hard places. I'm not so bitter anymore.

Chapter Fifteen

I can't think about that right now.
If I do, I'll go crazy. I'll think about that tomorrow.

—Scarlett O'Hara in *Gone with the Wind*

We never took tomorrow for granted in the Sisterhood. When Becca brought this quote to us one night, we voted to make "I'll Think About It Tomorrow" our official motto. We talked about having T-shirts made with this new motto on the back and our name, Sisterhood of the Dropped Stitches, on the front.

No matter how bad it got, we could always bring a smile to each others' faces by suggesting that we think about it tomorrow. Having a tomorrow was a good thing; we each wanted all of them we could get.

I haven't written in the journal since Monday, but I want you to know that my dad is coming through for us. It's late Wednesday afternoon, and he's got everything organized for tonight. He's at the dealership now so that the guys from the fire department where Lizabett's brothers work can haul eighty chairs over to the showroom when they finish their shift in an hour or so. They're good guys. The fire department is loaning us the chairs. Even more good.

We're planning to have a party here at The Pews after the performance tonight. Cast and audience are all invited. Buffalo wings and taquitos on the house. Uncle Lou put a notice on the outside door that there will be a private party here at nine o'clock tonight so we'll be closed to the public. I have bunches of pink and white balloons in my office that I plan to bring out and scatter around.

I haven't seen Quinn since Monday when he brought by the swan wings for Lizabett. I know he's been working long shifts, because Lizabett has dropped that information in my lap several times. I finally figured out that she's nervous about Quinn and me. I need to tell her that she doesn't need to worry about us because there is no us, but she never lets me get the words out of my mouth.

I think I have disappointed Quinn. I've been hoping he will invite me to go to the performance with him tonight—not so that it would be a date, I've learned my lesson there—but just because I want to watch his face as he sees Lizabett dance around in the ballet.

But, since Quinn hasn't actually talked to me lately, I don't think it's likely he'll be inviting me anywhere.

I have given up on meeting my dating goal by Thursday, that's tomorrow, and the amazing thing is that Becca has let me. Carly and Lizabett will meet their goals, and that will have to be enough for all of us, since Becca won't know if she's accepted for the other internship until next week at the earliest.

I'm trying to keep a happy expression on my face, but I am obviously not succeeding. There's no other reason I can think of that would explain why Becca is not pounding at me to meet my goal. She must feel sorry for me.

That should bother me and I'm sure it will in a couple of days. For now, I feel sorry enough for me that I don't even blame her.

The only one who doesn't feel sorry for me is Carly, and she looks as though she's got the world on her own shoulders, so I'm more inclined to feel sorry for her than to expect sympathy from her. I don't even know why she's so upset. All she will say is that the roses she got for her aunt didn't work. I never even knew she had an aunt close by until she told us that's why she bought the roses.

Oh, well, you don't want to hear about our troubles, so I'm going to sign off for a little bit. I'll pick it up after the performance so I can let you know how it went.

Hi, this is Lizabett. I'm sneaking in here for a second to let you know it's going to happen! Pinch me! I'm going to glide around like a swan in front of the lights!! It's my dream come true. I never thought we'd pull it all together—the lights were a little tricky, but we rented some. I'm so excited.

I'm even planning a small speech for the party after the ballet tonight. Can you imagine that? Me neither, but I want to thank Marilee and my brothers for all they have done—and Marilee's dad, of course. I can't wait.

Oh, and I'm trying to arrange the numbers on the chairs so that Quinn and Marilee will have seats together. I asked Quinn if he wanted me to get him a chair beside Marilee and he said she should sit with her date. The guy is deaf—I have told him Marilee doesn't have a date at least ten times. But he doesn't seem to believe me. I don't know what to do with him.

Well, this is Marilee. I just opened the journal and read what Lizabett wrote. I guess I was supposed to read it—it wasn't folded down or anything, it was right there for me to see. I'm not sure what Lizabett plans to gain by pointing out to Quinn that I don't have a date. I think the Sisterhood has become a little obsessed with my dating life. Don't you think?

Well, and Quinn is oblivious to me—he's

clearly not paying any attention to my life if he thinks I'm running around dating someone.

I don't know if I will be able to talk Lizabett out of juggling the seats, but I should try. I don't want to *force* Quinn to sit beside me.

Fortunately, I had to come back from the dealership to get some tape. My dad and I are supposed to tape numbered tags on the folding chairs so everyone will have reserved seating. It's been kind of nice to work together, the two of us. Anyway, if I could find the master list of who goes with what chair number, I wouldn't need to talk to Lizabett to see if the seating arrangements have been, well, further arranged by her while I've been over here.

I think I'll take the journal with me so you can get my updates as they happen. Besides, that way no one else will be able to leave a little message for me this way.

Ah, I meant to check in sooner. But things have been busy and I'm just now taking a breather. This is Marilee, by the way. The chairs have all been set up and the stage is being arranged. There are lots of plants and some plywood settings that look pretty good actually.

Quinn is in charge of the costumes, and he's buried under a mound of swan wings. I'm going to go over and ask him if he needs any help before I leave.

I think I have the seating situation under control. I don't know who I'm sitting next to, but I saw that someone had moved my ticket—I'm assuming that was Lizabett—so I just moved myself over to the other side of the room. I couldn't tell which ticket belonged to Quinn—or anyone else really, but I think I'm sitting beside Becca now. My dad is sitting across from us with Uncle Lou.

I'm going to check with Quinn and then run back to my office for a little bit and get dressed up for the performance. I won't be adding to the journal until after the performance. Do you know that this showroom still has that new car smell even though all of the cars have been taken out? I wish you could smell it. It's nice.

This is the intermission and I'm back—it's Marilee. I wasn't going to write anything until the end of the performance, but I figured it wouldn't hurt to give you a brief update while the dancers take a bit of a break and the audience stands and stretches.

The ballet is wonderful. And I'm going to tell you about that—but first, I'm going to tell you that I'm no match for Lizabett. She must have seen me move my seating number, because she moved Quinn over to sit next to me. I should have known better. One should never underestimate a Sister.

Quinn didn't seem surprised to see me sitting there when he found his assigned seat.

"I could move," Quinn said the minute he sat down.

The lights had not gone down to signal the beginning of the production yet, but everyone else was settled.

"We're fine," I said.

Whoever had set up our short row of folding chairs had squeezed us between a wall and a ficus tree that marked the beginning of the stage. I couldn't sit in my chair without having my arm pressed fully against Quinn's arm unless I wanted to sit on the lap of the woman on the other side of me—who, as it turned out, was the mother of one of the other ballet students.

"Sorry," I said when I tried, unsuccessfully, to make more room for Quinn.

Quinn just grunted. "I guess Randy was supposed to sit here. His shoulders aren't as wide."

"What?"

"I saw you move the numbers earlier," Quinn said. "Figured you were trying to sit by him so you could get in another date before tomorrow."

"I don't want to sit by Randy."

Quinn lifted his eyebrow. "Why not? At least you count *his* dates as dates."

"What are you talking about?"

"I heard you said he was your one date so far."

Oh, I see what the problem is. And it makes me feel better than I have since Monday. "It's not that his date counted more—it was just more clearly a date."

The lights were dimming, and there was some music starting to play.

"What's that supposed to mean?" Quinn growled at me softly.

"Well, you're my friend," I whispered back at him. The music was rising, and it was almost time for the dancers to come on stage. "I didn't want to use you, so I didn't want to count the time we spent together as dates because I didn't really know if they were dates."

"I kissed you," Quinn whispered indignantly in my ear. The dancers were on stage and it was time for quiet. He reached over and took my hand. "If that doesn't make something a date, I don't know what does."

"Oh. I thought you were just being nice."

"Nice!" Quinn's voicc rosc cnough that the woman sitting on the other side of him turned to frown.

"This is nice," Quinn whispered as he settled my hand in his.

We couldn't talk anymore because the music was soaring music. The ballet had begun.

I was right to want to watch Quinn's face while he followed his sister's performance. Lizabett dipped and swirled. She was amazing. And Quinn was so proud.

At the intermission, Quinn had to help sew one of the swan's wings back on, so he had to leave. That's why I took time to let you know that the ballet was going very well. My dad waved at me from across the stage where he was sitting with Uncle Lou and Rose. He was clearly enjoying himself. And I see Carly over there, sitting between Randy and Becca.

Then Quinn came back.

"What's this?" I asked, seeing the strip of white felt that Quinn had in his hands.

"Oh, I put felt on the wings so they won't rub anyone when they strap them around their arms."

"You're the one," I said to him.

"That's what I've been trying to tell you," he chuckled.

"No, I mean, you're the one who put felt on those crowns Lizabett brought to us when the Sisterhood first started meeting."

Quinn shrugged. "The cardboard was scratchy."

That seemed to be the end of the story to him. If something needed to be done, he would do it without fanfare or thanks.

I wondered if he even knew what a special man he is.

Two minutes into the second half of the

ballet, Quinn took my hand again and snuggled it into his own.

"This is another thing that makes a date," Quinn whispered in my ear as he squeezed my hand.

"That it does," I whispered as I squeezed his hand back.

Chapter Sixteen

There's no place like home.
—another Dorothy quote from
The Wizard of Oz

Uncle Lou was smart when he set up the meeting room for the Sisterhood like a living room. We all craved the warmth that came from sitting in a home together. We moved from the hospital conference room to The Pews a month or so after we started to meet. We all swore our knitting improved when we made the move. I was not convinced that was true. It seemed to me that we talked more and knitted less when we sat in our room at The Pews. But it didn't bother me—I had already decided I'd rather have fewer scarves and more friends so talking was good with me.

It's almost time for me, Marilee, to pass the journal on to someone else in the Sisterhood, but I want to tell you about our Thursday meeting before I do that. Last night's party had gone until midnight, and all of the ballet dancers had a great time—as did those of us in the audience.

My dad and Uncle Lou even led us all in singing some old songs from the sixties. I had no idea either one of them could sing that well.

Because of the party, I wasn't surprised that I didn't hear from any of the Sisters during the day. I was certainly busy enough myself that I didn't have time to e-mail them. I had three, count them—one, two, three dates.

Quinn had the day off and so he began with breakfast. He knew I was planning to go to Pastor Engstrom's meeting so he went with me. I don't mind telling you that the meeting was an eye-opener for me. There's more to being a Christian than I ever imagined, and I'm going to talk with my mom about it more before next week.

Anyway, the meeting was over by nine, and Quinn took me to Marston's for their crunchy French toast topped with fresh berries and real maple syrup.

Of course, Quinn had to kiss me when he brought me back to my office. He said he didn't want me to have any doubt that we had just been on a date. I could barely concentrate on ordering supplies in the two hours we had until lunch.

For lunch, he came back and took me to the Tea Room at the Huntington Gardens for scones and little watercress and salmon sandwiches. That time, Quinn kissed me in the middle of the bamboo grove down between the Japanese and the desert gardens.

He didn't even bother to take me back to The Pews after lunch. We just strolled around the gardens until it closed at five.

Then it was time for an early dinner, he said, which had to be special so he took me to the new French restaurant that opened up just over the bridge in Eagle Rock. That time he kissed me in the parking lot before we drove back to Pasadena.

If I didn't need to be here for the Sisterhood meeting, we would still be sitting in that parking lot. I told Quinn I was okay with missing the meeting, but he insisted I be here to officially record that I had met my goal.

Lizabett is the first one to show up for the meeting and she squeals and hugs Quinn when she sees him sitting at a table in the main part of the diner. They talk for a minute and I know he's told her about the dates, because her face is all rosy when she comes into the Sisterhood room.

Carly is the next Sister to arrive and, between you and me, she still looks as though things aren't going well for her. Lizabett and I both give her hugs and I ask how it's going, but she just shrugs.

Then Rose and Becca come in together. I wonder if Rose and Becca have been having a talk about how important, or unimportant, it is that we were able to meet the goals we set a year ago.

I'm reassured that Becca is okay with us not all meeting our goals when I see that she has brought four candles so that we can light a candle for each successful goal reached.

"But a candle will keep," she says. "We'll just wait and light it when that goal is reached."

"Marilee reached her goal," Lizabett says. "Three dates with my brother, Quinn. Lunch, breakfast and dinner."

I get three surprised looks and then three big grins.

"Way to go," Becca says as she rushes over to give me a hug.

"So it's Quinn," Rose says as she hugs me, too.

"That's wonderful," Carly says, and her face looks happy.

We light the three candles for Carly, Lizabett and me and turn off the overhead light in the room.

I must say I look around at my friends sitting here with a feeling of extreme satisfaction.

"It's a good time tonight to turn over the journal to someone else," I say after we've all had a few moments of quiet reflection.

"But it's your journal," Lizabett protests.

I hold up the journal. It's no longer a smooth notebook—instead, it's worn and lumpy with all those folded and clipped pages. "You can see it's not just one person's journal. The story of the Sisterhood belongs to all of us."

"Carly should go next," Becca says suddenly.

"Oh, I don't—" Carly protests.

I nod. Maybe having the journal will help Carly figure out what is wrong. I know it helped me think through my problems with my father and with God, too. I think some of the bitterness drained away when I wrote it down on these pages.

We all agree that Carly will take the journal next.

"I don't know if I'll say the right things," Carly says.

"There is no wrong thing to say."

"Don't worry, we'll add our opinions here and there, too," Becca says. "Just to be sure you're on track."

"I'll hand it over as soon as I finish writing about today's meeting," I say even as I get my pen out.

I can't write too well by candlelight, but I don't have too much to say before I pass the journal on anyway so I will keep it simple. I am a blessed woman. I no longer think that

God dropped any stitches when He made me. I haven't quite wrapped my mind all around it, but I think Pastor Engstrom might be right about God loving me. Isn't that something?

Added to that, I am just getting used to the fact that my dad might care about me more than I had thought and that maybe Quinn even has feelings for me that are a little bit more than friendship—if you had been there for the kissing parts, you would know that's true.

Well, you can see why I say I am blessed. I can look through the windows and into the main part of The Pews where Quinn is sitting, waiting for me. He's a good man. I know I only needed three dates to meet my goal, but I'm wondering if Quinn might not like to go a little further and have a fourth date today. A stroll down to the Colorado Bridge would be romantic. We could even have another kiss or two under the stars. Now, that would be nice.

* * * * *

Dear Reader,

The reason I wrote *The Sisterhood of the Dropped Stitches* is that I wanted to write about a group of young women who have become friends—sisters, even—in the hard times of life. These are the kinds of friends you can call on no matter what. I'm sure many of you have (and are) friends like that. I hope this book encourages you in those friendships.

As I wrote this book, I found myself constantly asking myself what a good friend would do in a certain situation. Would she be nosy? Yes, sometimes. Would she be too pushy once in a while? Yes, probably. Would she be perfect? Maybe—for *brief* periods of time. What she would be, I decided, is by her friend's side—whether or not she agreed with her friend, whether or not it was easy, she'd be there.

The American Breast Cancer Foundation recommends women over:

Age 20: Should perform self breast exams each month. Have a clinical breast exam at least every two years.

Age 40: Should perform self breast exams each month. Have a clinical breast exam and a mammogram at least every year.

I hope you enjoy *The Sisterhood of the Dropped Stitches*. And may you have many good friends.

Blessings,

Janet Tronstad

QUESTIONS FOR DISCUSSION

1. The four main characters each responded to their cancer in different ways. Think of a time in your life when it seemed like you were singled out for hard times. Which Sisterhood character's response is closest to your response? (see below)

Becca—She believed in telling it as it was, no matter how unpleasant the "it" might be.

Carly—She knew what she faced, right down to the numbers on her blood test. She just always thought everything would be okay.

Lizabett—She was too shy sometimes to even find out what she needed to know from the nurses or the lab techs.

Marilee—The resentment about how unfair her life had become festered in her. She used to wonder if God had been watching some landmark football game on television when He made us and that was why He missed the stitches that ended up letting cancer into our bodies.

2. Extreme hardship (such as cancer) can also bring blessings along with the pain. What blessings did you find for the members of the Sisterhood, both during and after their battle with cancer? What blessings have you found in your own life in hard times?

3. Have you ever been in a tight-knit, small group like the Sisterhood of the Dropped Stitches? If so, what was your experience?
4. Marilee struggled with her relationship with her father and felt he did not care enough about her cancer. How did this affect her relationship with God?
5. Lizabett also struggled in the opposite way with her oldest brother, "The Old Mother Hen." Have you ever had someone worry too much about you? Do you think that would affect someone's relationship with God, as well? In what ways?
6. Thinking about your own struggles in life, have they drawn you closer to God? How?
7. The Sisterhood decide to share their story with others. Do you share your struggles with others? Where and how do you do this? What is the result of this sharing?
8. Do you think churches do enough to help people who are sick deal with their spiritual questions? What more could we all do?

Turn the page for a sneak peek at
Janet Tronstad's next book,
A Match Made in Dry Creek,
available in April 2007.

Chapter One

Winter and guilt didn't go well together in a place like Dry Creek, Montana, not even for Mrs. Hargrove, who, after decades of living there, was used to the icy snow that sometimes forced a person with unsure footing to stay home for days at a time with nothing more than her own thoughts for company.

Mrs. Hargrove had lived her life with few regrets, so she generally spent those days peacefully chopping vegetables for soup or putting together thousand-piece puzzles. This past winter, though, she hadn't been able to do either of those things. Her conscience was troubling her, and she lacked the focus needed to figure out a puzzle or decide what needed to go into a pot of soup.

Instead, she sat and stared at the pictures on the mantel over her fireplace. There was the picture of her and her late husband, taken on their wedding day. And then there was a picture of her daughter, Doris June, taken when she graduated from high school. It wasn't a particularly good picture, because even though Doris June was smiling, her eyes looked sad and she had acquired a certain stiffness in her face that Mrs. Hargrove hadn't noticed until she sat and studied the picture. For years Mrs. Hargrove had expected to exchange that picture of Doris June for a glowing wedding picture of her daughter on her wedding day.

But that wedding had never come. Doris June was still single and looked set to stay that way. It was a heartache to Mrs. Hargrove that Doris June had shown little interest in marriage, but she couldn't say anything. Mrs. Hargrove knew it was her fault that her daughter wasn't married so she only sat and brooded over those pictures. When it was time to eat, she didn't have the appetite to do more than open a can of soup, scarcely paying attention to what the label said.

The one huge mistake Mrs. Hargrove had made in her life had come back to haunt her, and she couldn't stop fretting about it. Of course, she prayed about it. Every night. But even with all the prayer, she couldn't shake the feeling that she needed to do something more.

The problem had come back to mind in early January when she and Charley Nelson had sat down at her kitchen table to begin writing a history of their small town. The two of them were the oldest of the two hundred some residents of Dry Creek, and when the state tourism board asked the town to write a section for an upcoming guide book, everyone said she and Charley were the natural ones to write it. Mrs. Hargrove and Charley agreed to do the work, thinking it would be a good way for them to pass the cold winter months pleasantly.

It didn't take them long to realize how wrong they had been. They knew it as soon as they opened the large envelope from the state tourism board. Mrs. Hargrove and

Charley had not known until that moment that the guide book was being called *Stop at One-Stop-Sign Towns in Southern Montana.* Each town was supposed to begin their two pages of history and visitor attractions with an opening paragraph telling what made their particular old red Stop sign unique.

It was the sign that was the problem.

The one Stop sign in Dry Creek was at the south end of town next to the Enger home place. Twenty-five years ago two local teenagers had hit that sign with an old blue pickup as they were beginning their elopement to Las Vegas. The passenger side of that pickup had bent the sign post until it looked like the smashed half of a Valentine heart. Both being responsible individuals, the teens reported the damage to the sheriff, who then called their parents—from there, everything spun out of control until eventually the eloping couple were torn apart.

No one knew whether it was the broken heart shape of the sign or the gossip about the two star-crossed teens, but the story of that Stop sign was told and re-told that year until it became as close to a legend as anything Dry

Creek had. A few years later a local musician had written a song about the heart sign, and it had played on the radio for a while, so that people here and there throughout the state knew the story. The tourism staff had obviously heard of that sign.

Even today, someone would periodically place fresh flowers at the base of the rusted sign or carve their initials on the bent post. The sign itself had two bullet holes that had been shot into the "O" of the "Stop" years ago. Back then, local teenagers said those two holes were like two arrows shot straight into the heart of true love.

Every once in a while, there was talk of fixing the sign or pulling it down altogether, since the intersection it guarded was scarcely used any longer. But no one could quite make the decision to disturb the sign after its crooked form had become part of the heart of Dry Creek itself.

Charley had his elbows on Mrs. Hargrove's worn oak table and his right hand was curled around a cup of her fine brewed coffee. The contents of the envelope were sitting in front of him on the table. "Of course, everyone who was here twenty-five years ago knew it was Doris June and Curt who were on their way to Las Vegas to elope when they hit that sign—so it's not like anything was a secret even back then."

Doris June was Mrs. Hargrove's daughter. Curt was Charley's son.

Mrs. Hargrove winced. "If things had turned out differently, the story of them and that sign would be a funny family story—just the kind of thing we'd laugh about as we bounced our grandbabies on our knees." Mrs. Hargrove stopped to sigh. She had no grandchildren. "But, as it is, I doubt either Curt or Doris June would like to see a reminder of that day in print anywhere, and I'm not sure I have the stomach for it either."

"What else could we do? Doris June had just turned seventeen. I wanted her to go to college and have a chance at the world. Was that so wrong? You know I didn't object to Curt himself, it was just the timing of things."

"Me, too. I loved Doris June like the daughter I never had," Charley said. "But I thought I was being a good parent. What did two seventeen-year-old kids know about getting married?"

"They were too young," Mrs. Hargrove said, and Charley nodded.

Neither one of them said much more. Mrs. Hargrove offered Charley some oatmeal raisin cookies to go with his coffee and he only ate two, explaining his appetite just wasn't with him. Mrs. Hargrove said she understood.

The information for the guide book wasn't due until June so Mrs. Hargrove and Charley decided to let the matter rest for a while.

Over the next couple of months, Mrs. Hargrove's mind kept going back to that fateful day when the Nelson parents and the Hargrove parents had forbidden their children to marry.

Mrs. Hargrove knew she and her late husband had good intentions just like the Nelsons had. Mrs. Hargrove thought she was doing the best thing by sending Doris June off to Anchorage to live with her aunt and refusing to give Curt the aunt's address when he asked for it.

Mrs. Hargrove had no idea Doris June would never marry and that Curt would get so angry with his folks for interfering that he'd sign up with the army just to leave home and then later make a disaster of the one marriage he entered into.

As the winter wore on, Mrs. Hargrove and Charley felt so bad about the mess they'd made of things all those years ago that they could barely face each other. Finally, they both knew something had to be done to set things right again.

"If we could un-match them back then we should be able to match them up again now," Charley finally said.